THE YOUNG BOSS
OF CAMP EIGHTEEN

THE YOUNG BOSS
OF CAMP EIGHTEEN

ERNEST L. THURSTON

Originally published in 1934.

Published by Wildside Press.

Visit us online at wildsidepress.com.

INTRODUCTION
KARL WURF

Ernest L. Thurston (1873-1958) was a Massachusetts-born writer who carved out a distinctive niche in the golden age of American juvenile adventure fiction. Writing primarily in the 1930s, Thurston specialized in outdoor adventure stories that combined wilderness survival, industrial settings, and moral character development—themes that resonated with young readers during the Depression era when self-reliance and practical skills held particular appeal.

His Black Shadow series (also known as the Young Heroes series), published by Akron, Ohio's Saalfield Publishing Company, consisted of three novels following the adventures of Walter Northrop and his companions through the lumber camps and wilderness of the North Woods. The series takes its name from Lupus, the magnificent wolf-dog owned by Raoul Rigaud, one of Walter's closest friends. The trilogy begins with *The Black Shadow*, continues with *The Young Boss of Camp Eighteen*, and concludes with *Tongues of Flame*, in which Walter and his friends prospect timber while solving the mystery of forest fires threatening both the Northrop holdings and those of a rival company. Together, the three books form a complete arc of Walter's development from adventurous youth to capable young leader in his father Big Jim's lumber empire.

Thurston's work emerged during an extraordinarily fertile period for juvenile series fiction. The late 1920s and 1930s saw the launch of two cultural phenomena that would define young readers' literature for generations: The Hardy Boys debuted in 1927, followed by Nancy Drew in 1930, both from the Stratemeyer Syndicate's prolific factory of juvenile mysteries. These series, along with dozens of competitors, established the template of recurring teenage protagonists solving mysteries and having adventures with minimal adult supervision—a formula that proved irresistible to young readers seeking excitement and independence, even if only vicariously through the pages of a book.

What distinguished Thurston's Black Shadow trilogy from the mystery-focused Hardy Boys or Nancy Drew was its emphasis on authentic outdoor skills and industrial settings. While Frank and Joe Hardy raced roadsters and pursued smugglers, and Nancy Drew solved mysteries in her fashionable convertible, Walter Northrop learned to fell timber, read animal tracks, and manage rough-hewn lumberjacks in sub-zero blizzards. Thurston's novels offered a more rugged, physically demanding world where survival skills mattered as much as cleverness, and where the protagonist had to earn respect through demonstrated competence rather than simply being naturally gifted at detection.

The lumber camp setting also reflected an America that was rapidly disappearing. By the 1930s, the great North Woods logging operations were already in decline, giving Thurston's vivid descriptions of camp life, timber drives, and wilderness survival a nostalgic quality even for contemporary readers. His detailed attention to logging terminology, techniques, and camp hierarchy suggests either personal familiarity with the industry or meticulous research—the kind of authenticity that elevated his work above simple pulp adventure.

In *The Young Boss of Camp Eighteen*, the second book in the trilogy, Thurston presents Walter Northrop's coming-of-age as a test of leadership under pressure. The seventeen-year-old must prove himself to skeptical, battle-hardened woodsmen while simultaneously uncovering an industrial sabotage conspiracy. The novel combines the workplace realism of books like *Captains Courageous* with the mystery elements of the Hardy Boys, all set against the authentic backdrop of Depression-era logging operations. The result is a vigorous adventure that speaks to timeless themes: earning respect, facing danger with courage, and standing by your friends when the stakes are highest.

For modern readers, Thurston's work offers a window into both the juvenile literature of the 1930s and the vanished world of industrial logging. His prose is straightforward and action-driven, designed to keep pages turning, while his moral framework—emphasizing loyalty, self-reliance, and earned authority—reflects the values of his era. The Black Shadow trilogy may not have achieved the enduring fame of the Stratemeyer Syndicate's creations, but it represents an authentic and entertaining strand of American adventure fiction that deserves rediscovery by readers interested in wilderness tales, historical industry, or the evolution of young adult literature.

CHAPTER I
In the Grip of the Blizzard

As THE TRAIN JARRED to a halt beside a wooden shelter, marking a wayside stop, the blizzard took it in its teeth and shook it until its windows rattled. The light day coach trembled and rocked under the buffets of the howling northwest gale that blew unobstructed across an open field. Clouds of snow and grit, wind driven, spattered like hail against the windowpanes. Icy air and fine snow powder sifted through cracks and crevices. The lone passenger who disembarked was instantly caught in the grip of the gusts and sent staggering down a road until he faded from sight in the snow curtain.

"*Br-r-r-r!*" Donald Atkinson shivered, despite his heavy sweater and Mackinaw coat. His teeth chattered. "D-do they think w-we n-need to be r-refrigerated? The r-r-radiator p-p-pipes are s-stone c-cold. I-I'm beginning to w-wish I'd n-never c-come."

Walter Northrop, a tall, lithe chap with sandy hair, chuckled amusedly. "You've less right to complain than the rest of us, Don. You've flesh enough on that stocky frame of yours to keep you warm." He glanced out the window, and his keen gray eyes sparkled as if he enjoyed the storm. "It must be some job, Don, for the fireman to keep steam up against the blizzard. And what he does get is needed to keep the locomotive bucking the drifts."

"I feel," laughed Clement Osgood, a slight, wiry, dark-haired chap, "that Don ought to lend us slim fellows his sweater, at least."

"Just let me s-see you try to t-take it," snapped Don, in no way appeased. "I may have m-more flesh, but it's just s-so m-much more to g-get cold." He burrowed deeper into his collar.

"Think we'll make Base Station all right, Walt?" inquired Clement.

"No can tell, Clem," answered Walter. A faint trace of anxiety flashed across his face and was gone. "We've only a light locomotive, and the drifts are deepening steadily. We may stall in some of the cuts up ahead."

"At least," exclaimed Clement, "if we *never* get there, it will have been worth trying, just for the experience of this storm."

With spinning wheels and roaring exhaust, the engine backed its two-car train a couple of hundred yards, stopped, and then went ahead with gradually increasing speed. The group of boys, having learned from experience, braced themselves. A moment later there came a shock as the engine rammed a drift. It jarred and pounded but broke through. They moved on. Again forest growth shut them in on either side. Then, once more, speed decreased and they came to a halt on the edge of a slight cut. They backed down the track.

"If she stalls," growled Donald, "I stay with her if I have to hibernate all winter."

"Without food for at least twenty-four hours, let alone the whole period?" queried Walter.

"Wow! I never thought of that." Donald swallowed, and an expression of distress dawned on his face. "Gee! Just the mention of that makes me hungry. *That* puts a different complexion on the matter. To prevent such a catastrophe, I'd get out and shove."

"Better yet," chuckled Clement, "go up front and break a path for that puffing railbird that's hauling us."

Progress, a succession of backs and bucks, became slower and slower. They were running, now, into slightly rolling country. Cuts were multiplying. Despite the snow fences erected to guard them, snow was blowing over their tops and filling in the depths. With increasing difficulty the train battered its way through several of these snow traps and rolled into a short stretch of more open country where the gale had swept the tracks clear. Speed increased for a minute or so, then checked and ended as they ran into a curving defile. Again the train reversed direction.

"I'm fed up with this frog-in-the-well business," growled Donald, yet with a faint grin.

The train lunged forward and hit the snow pack. Glancing slantingly forward through the windows, the boys could see snow masses shoot high in air and then travel away in the grip of the wind. At once a stop and a labored backing.

"First down," murmured Clement.

Still again, with a harder shock than before, they rammed the packed snow plug.

"Second down, four yards to go," contributed Donald, really grinning this time. His grouchy moods seldom lasted long. "Six yards nearer sausages and pancakes."

"*Brace hard!*" snapped Walter. "This will be the worst yet."

The train had backed again, farther down the track this time. It picked up more speed as it charged forward. There was a sudden tremendous jar. An almost instant stop followed with such unexpectedness that Donald, who had not taken the warning seriously, was catapulted into the aisle. A windowpane shattered, and fragments of glass showered down on him. Icy air flooded in.

"Who tackled me?" demanded Donald, picking himself up and rubbing his head. "No gain. Let's try a forward pass."

"Trouble up front, I'm afraid," said Walter soberly.

So it proved. In a few minutes the harassed-looking conductor appeared. His face was raw and bleeding from the sand-papering of snow and ice particles. Icicles adorned his mustache.

"Stalled," he announced gloomily to the handful of passengers. "Our fore-truck jumped the track that time. Our coal's low; our sand is about out. Moreover, the rotary is broken down somewhere up the line. Looks like we might be tied up here for twenty-four hours, seems if. There's a farmhouse a mile back on the left, and the track won't drift deep for an hour. Some of you may wish to try for it."

Exclaiming and complaining, some of the passengers began bestirring themselves. But in the act of checking over the belongings of his own group Walter paused and touched the conductor's arm.

"Isn't Valley Highway near here?" he asked. "As I recall, there's a crossroads store there."

"Two miles, Son, but you'd not make it. Near-zero weather and a rip-snorting fifty-mile gale! All drifted over ahead, deep! Don't be a fool!"

"I ought to get ahead," responded Walter. "I must get to Base Station, somehow, as soon as possible. We've some snowshoes with our dunnage in your express car. We could get them, I suppose. As to the trip, I was brought up in this region and know how to take care of myself. I'd like to try it, if you'll lend me a train ax. Might come in handy if we have to make shelter. I'll leave it for you at some station up the road."

"I reckon that's all right, if you're sure you know your business." The conductor eyed him sharply. "Seems's if I've seen you. You look like Jim Northrop's son."

"I am," responded Walter proudly.

"Then you're the son of the best woodsman in the state. There ain't no lumberman to beat Big Jim. You can be trusted, too. I've heard of you."

"Thank you, sir!" said Walter, coloring. He turned to his companions. "Are you game, fellows? It will be tough going. But you know how important it is for me to reach Camp Eighteen ahead of the gang."

"Of course," spoke up Clement grittily, "if you'll rig up some sort of anchor to keep me from blowing away."

"Just tie up to me," grinned Donald. "I'm going. That is, assuming there's a hot meal at the end of the trail." He turned. "But, Walt, how will our going to this store you speak of help you in getting to Camp Eighteen? We'll just be holed in there, instead of here?"

Walter grinned. "You see," he responded, "I intended to stock up with provisions and then trail away on our snowshoes. This branch road may not be dug out for days."

"In this?" Donald waved his hand at the vicious tempest.

"This blizzard will blow itself out tonight," said Walter. "We'll be able to make it."

"Sure we can," agreed Clement.

Donald nodded, but rather soberly.

"Knew I could count on you chaps." Walter flashed a smile at them. "Wait here. I'm taking our grips forward. They'll follow us. I'll get out our snowshoes and the stuff we must have with us."

In fifteen minutes he was back with the shoes and with three light turkeys, or duffel bags, arranged to slip over their necks. Laughing and joking, the boys buttoned their coats tight, fastened down the flaps of their fur caps, slipped their bags over their heads, caught up their snowshoes, and headed for the door. On the way, Walter appropriated the ax from its wall case.

All being ready, he signaled the others, opened the door, and stepped out on the platform of the old-fashioned coach. His companions followed just as a wild blast roared in. It sent Walter and Donald staggering against the rail and tossed the lighter Clement bodily off the car and head first into a snowdrift. The others leaped down and jerked him out, kicking and gasping.

"Don't talk, fellows," snapped Walter. "Mouths closed. Save your breath. Follow me."

He led the way along the protected side of the train, then turned off and broke a path through heavy drifts into a near-by belt of spruce woods. It was tough going, for the snow was both deep and loose. Both Clement and Donald were winded by the time they stopped in the shelter of the thick growth. Walter, however, appeared unaffected.

"The trees break the wind and prevent much drifting," he said. "Now we'll put on our shoes and make a real start. I'll break trail and you follow in my tracks. Only, watch your steps. There will be all sorts of things just under the snow to trip you up."

Presently he set off, slowly and methodically, breaking trail. The others alternated at his heels. After five minutes he stopped, allowed two minutes for rest, and then went on again. His companions were far less experienced travelers on snowshoes than he. They stumbled and tripped and fell frequently. And when they cut across open spaces the full force of the gale bowled them over or drove them far off the line of march.

By the time the first mile had been covered, Clement and Donald were staggering from weariness. Difficulty in breathing the icy air had made it hard for them to get their second wind. Walter eyed them closely several times. Finally he led them into dense woods, stopping when he came upon an immense boulder. Swinging around to the sheltered side, he motioned to his companions to rest.

At once Walter clipped a bough from a near-by spruce and brushed the snow from a small area of ground. Then he took his ax, stepped over to a standing dead birch and felled it with a few well-placed blows. Lopping off the branches, he began chopping the trunk into short lengths.

Seeing what was coming, Clement immediately got busy breaking off and collecting brittle dead twigs. He had these heaped up and ablaze by the time Walter began bringing over branches and his short cuts. In a few minutes a hot fire was roaring.

"Coats off," snapped Walter. "Let the heat penetrate way in. Now for refreshments." With a grin at Donald, he took from his pocket a number of packages of chocolate.

"*Geewillikers!*" gasped Donald. "If I'd known you had those, there would have been a hold-up long before this. *Gimme!* I'm dying of starvation."

Clement and Walter exchanged grins, but all munched their bars with relish while they basked in the warmth of the blaze. It was hard to realize, with the fire in front and the rock at their backs, how severe a blizzard was raging. The others felt ready for anything long before Walter gave the signal to move. So they sat back lazily talking over past experiences and discussing the weeks immediately before them.

The three were chums who were planning to continue their education together through engineering and forestry schools. Walter, as the son of a great lumberman, was already an expert woodsman and timber cruiser. He was familiar, from actual experience, with the common processes of lumbering. But his companions had gained their main woods experience only in two outings under his guidance.

During the fall, a little over a year before, the three had made an excursion into the woods to take pictures of wild animals. The taking of these pictures had led to many exciting adventures, including the running down of a giant moose—the Spirit Moose.

But interwoven with these adventures had been the working out of a mysterious message and the search for and rescue of a young chap, Raoul Rigaud. Raoul had broken his leg while alone in the woods and had managed to exist only through the help of The Black Shadow, his famous wolf dog.

The second woods experience had covered the entire following summer. The three boys, accompanied by Raoul, had made a special trip into the deep woods to cruise some timber and had met with more than one adventure and obstacle which had bound them together. Following that, they had spent the remaining weeks on fire duty on the immense Northrop holdings. In desperate fights against the fire demon, and in meeting other situations that arose, the friendship between the four had been cemented into a lasting comradeship.

Now the three were headed for Camp Eighteen, the newest camp of the Northrop holdings, which they had seen take form the previous summer. Here Walter was to undertake his first practical test in actually running a camp as camp boss, and his friends were going along to assist him. Because of the exceptional mental and physical development they had shown as a result of their previous outings, no difficulty had been experienced in securing school permission to employ a period of winter and early spring in this way. They intended, so far as possible, to keep up with their studies.

At last Walter jumped to his feet and began putting out the fire, knocking out the flames and covering all embers with snow. Then all put on their coats, fastened down their cap flaps, and again took up their bags. At once Walter led the way on through the woods, keeping to shelter so far as possible. But after a little over a mile they broke out of a thicket to find themselves in a wide white strip that extended endlessly in either direction.

"Valley Highway," yelled Walter, above the shriek and roar of the storm. "Now for the real struggle! We've got to buck the blizzard for a quarter of a mile."

At once he stepped out and faced into the teeth of the gale. The others followed him. Instantly all realized that, compared with this, what had gone before was mere child's play. The storm appeared to shriek at them menacingly. The snow cut and almost blinded them. The icy breath of the blizzard penetrated their clothing with numbing effect. Again and again the wind brought them up standing. Now and then buffets sent them hurtling backward or tossed them into drifts. And there was not even the slightest shelter.

Grimly Walter led the way. Often he had to break through drifts that were waist deep. The struggle taxed his strength. His pace slowed down. Yet he moved steadily, methodically, with a minimum of effort. He planted his feet carefully. He leaned against the wind, stopping when to struggle hard against the blasts meant too great an expenditure of energy.

Behind him, his two companions staggered along, at first in Indian file, then, as they wearied, arm in arm for mutual support. They were beyond words, save that Clement found himself gasping under his breath, "I've *got* to keep up. One step—at a—time. One step——"

At long last, staggering and falling and picking themselves up, they passed under a line of wires and knew they had crossed the railroad. The store must be near. But the swirling snow curtains shut it wholly from view. Clement, slightest of the three, was wavering. Walter dropped back to his side, caught up his right arm, and pulled it around his own neck. At a sign to Donald the latter did the same with Clement's left arm. Heads down, three abreast, they staggered on. A step—a stop—another step! Where was the building? Suppose they went by!

Without warning, they hit some firm obstruction and crashed heavily. They looked up. The dim form of a framed structure loomed before them. They realized that they had stumbled upon a flight of steps that led to a porch. With stiffened fingers they clawed off their snowshoes and crawled and clambered up the snow-drifted flight, fumbled at a door that unexpectedly opened, and met a blast of delicious warm air. Clement went dizzy and toppled to the floor.

Instantly Walter ripped off his own coat and cap and kneeled beside his friend, relieving him of his wraps.

"Sorry—I was—a burden," gasped Clement.

"Darned plucky, I'll say," exclaimed Donald unexpectedly. "But I tell you one thing, Walt, we're not going to tramp into camp, and you know it. Enough is plenty, and we've had it."

Walter grinned. "Tomorrow is another day," he chuckled. He turned to the storekeeper who was standing beside them. "Howdy, Parkins! I'm Jim Northrop's son. Can you stake us to quarters for tonight, and can you stuff this chap—" he indicated Donald—"so he'll quit yawping about being hungry?"

"Surest thing," exclaimed Parkins. "You're Walt, aren't you? Jim Northrop's son is welcome any time. Glad of comp'ny. No trade for two days. I d'no about stuffin' f'r a chap of that size. Looks like he used aplenty. How about sassages 'nd pancakes 'nd apple pie?"

"Man, you're my friend for life!" yelped Donald. "When? How soon? I'm that hungry I can only gasp."

"I only wish you'd had 'em cooking as we came along," chuckled Walter. "Don would have sniffed the odor, and there would have been no holding him. Clem and I would simply have grabbed his arms, and he would have dragged us here. By the way, Parkins, are your phone wires down?"

"They was ridin' a half hour back. You c'n try."

Walter went to the old-fashioned instrument on the wall and finally secured a response. He called "Base Station."

A long wait resulted. And when Walter finally got his connection he evidently had considerable difficulty in being understood and in understanding. Finally he came back and joined the others around the red-hot drum heater. He dropped into a chair and gazed soberly out the window.

"Message from Dad waiting for me there," he said at last. "As near as I can make out, the men for Camp Eighteen will arrive on the twentieth. That gives us three days to connect."

"Well, they're not likely to find us there," laughed Donald.

"They'll find *me* there," said Walter firmly.

Donald gazed at him curiously. "Spill it, Walt. What's up?"

"Dad sent a postscript, saying, 'Watch your step'!"

"That means trouble, Walt?" asked Clement quietly.

"Looks like something's up," acknowledged Walter.

"*Bully!*" yelped Donald. "Exciting times are here again. We've always had 'em. I can hardly wait to get started. But not until after dinner," he added quickly, and so seriously that the others roared.

CHAPTER II
Plumbing the Depths

THE BOYS AWOKE, THE next morning, in their warm ell room over the kitchen, to find a brilliant sun shining in upon them and reflecting from an outside world of glittering white. So dazzling, indeed, was the reflection from the snow that the boys put on their goggles before venturing many glances out. The storm, it was evident, had continued on its way, but a fresh wind was piling ever higher the drifts of snow powder. The temperature, however, was rising markedly.

Dressing rapidly, the three hastened downstairs, drawn by the fragrance of bacon and rolls. And they found, despite their feasting of the night before, that sleep and crisp air had magically renewed their appetites. They praised the food so heartily that Mrs. Parkins blushed with pleasure.

The meal finally over, after helping had been piled on helping, Walter set an example to the others by bringing in armfuls of wood until their hostess cried "Enough." After that they cleared paths to out-buildings and performed other helpful chores. Only when these were done did they prepare their loads for the trip before them. Their turkeys were heavier, for provisions and sleeping bags had to be added. Also Walter purchased two axes in the store, leaving the one he had borrowed with Mr. Parkins, to be returned to the train conductor when the railway was cleared.

"Why not skis in place of snowshoes?" suggested Clement. "Seems to me they'd be easier to use and give us greater speed."

"The snow is too light," returned Walter. "Besides, we will go through much dense growth and over some rough ground. I think you'd find the long skis bothering you. You see, I'm not heading for Base Station. That would take us out of our way, since I am sure our private lumber railroad will be sealed by the snow for days. I am going to cut straight through the woods to Camp Seven. From there on—we'll see."

An hour later, with accounts settled and farewells uttered, the three set out down the highway, up which they had struggled so desperately the afternoon before. Now, with the wind at their back, progress was easier, though the drifts gave serious trouble. Frequently these were higher than their heads, and were broken through only at considerable expenditure of energy.

But shortly Walter swung off the drifted highway into the woods. Here, though underfoot obstructions were constant and resulted in many trips and falls, drifts were far less troublesome. With short but frequent rests, the boys pushed steadily deeper into the wilderness. Walter persistently kept the lead, for he knew far better than his companions what was likely to lie beneath the concealing snow blanket.

At noon, Walter called a halt out in the open, well away from cliffs, though these were visible near by. He prepared to build a fire.

"Say," exclaimed Donald, who had been fretting for some time because he wished to get close enough to the cliffs to examine the snow masses that overhung their tops, "why not camp near the foot of that wall, yonder?"

"Because," chuckled Walter, "I don't relish having tons of snow down my neck. Keep an eye that way and you may see things before lunch is over."

They got their blaze going, fixed cushions of thick spruce boughs, heated some beans, and settled down to rest comfortably as they ate. They talked little, for they were not yet broken in to tramping, and especially to the unnatural gait made necessary by snowshoes.

"Look!" snapped Walter. He pointed. "This end of that cliff!"

A drift on the cliff edge had extended over in an enormous lip. Suddenly this broke loose and fell with a soft "plop," making a great heap at the base. Minor breaks ran along the overhang for some distance.

"Nice little natural candle snuffer," laughed Donald. "I——"

"Listen!" exclaimed Walter. "Here comes the real thing. Watch that very steep slope back of that second cliff."

An odd murmuring sound seemed to come from the air, yet it was not exactly like the note of the wind. It grew louder, deeper, with a threatening undertone. High up on the steep slope a dark streak showed suddenly, steadily enlarging. In front of it, down-slope, a white billow seemed to form.

"She's coming down!" yelped Donald, springing excitedly to his feet.

The moving snow mass was swelling in size and coming faster with every passing second. Small tree growth in its course wavered, tilted; some went down. The murmuring undertone became a threatening roar. From out of that moving wall of snow, something large and dark leaped high and forward, to again bury itself in the snow cascade.

"A boulder!" exclaimed Clement excitedly.

Other stones and boulders shot out, only to leap to cover again. A larger tree, near the top of the cliff, snapped off with a sharp report, staggered along drunkenly for a little; then rolled over and was buried. The roaring mass reached the edge of the cliff.

"*Whoo-oo-oo-i-i-i-sh-sh!*" it cried and leaped into space. Snow, rocks, trees poured over and crashed to the ground far below. A cloud of fine snow grit enveloped the boys, though they were a hundred yards in the open; and an icy wind almost swept them from their feet. Then, almost instantly, the sound died away. The silence seemed startling.

"*Crickets!*" gasped Donald. He had gone a little white. "Suppose we had been lunching up under that cliff."

"When a slide comes you want to be somewhere else," said Walter soberly. "Let's be moving."

The others agreed, almost eagerly. Though, after all, the slide was a small one, compared to a real mountain avalanche, they felt just a bit shaken. It would be good to get going again.

They tramped on for several hours. The way grew rougher and steeper. They were working over a long high ridge, cut by many streams. Walter moved with exceeding care, sometimes prodding the ground before taking a forward step, especially when he came to watercourses. Many of these were not visible, save as threads of snow stretching away and bare of trees.

"Easy to go down farther than you expect," he said. "The snow drifts in and fills up the channels after the water freezes, as it has done on the surface under this bitter cold wave."

A half hour later, as the chill of late afternoon began to be felt, he stopped on a windswept rock to make a little fire in a crevice and heat some tea to warm them for the last stretch before they camped for the night. Near by a wide and open band of white stretched up-grade, broken only here and there by ridges of stone festooned with giant icicles.

"Gorge Brook," said Walter. "Runs in a deep stone channel for miles on miles."

He busied himself with the little fire while Clement prepared the tea. Suddenly the latter missed Donald and turned to look for him. He was close to the buried brook, staring up at the ledges that made waterfalls in summer.

"Not too close, Don," Clement called.

Walter whipped around. "Come back out of there, Don," he ordered, sharply.

Donald shrugged his shoulders. He hesitated. Then took one slight step forward as he peered upstream. Instantly, with a choked cry, he toppled over and lunged into the snow. It closed over him.

With one wild leap, Walter was at his turkey, pulling free a coil of tough hemp rope he had packed at the last moment.

"A tree ladder, Clem," he yelled. "Twenty—thirty feet deep. Seconds count."

As Clement leaped for an ax, Walter sprang towards the gorge edge, un-coiling the rope as he ran. Arriving at the lip of the drop, he looped one end of his rope around a near-by tree, fastening it securely. Then, with the utmost speed, he made two or three knots at intervals. As Clement's ax sounded the first blows, Walter flung the free end of his rope over side, got a good grip on it, and let himself down, hand over hand. He disappeared from view, the snow closing over him also.

Clement worked madly. Never had he felled a tall sapling so rapidly. De-spite the nerve strain he was under, he made every blow tell. He realized the danger below, in that gorge. That fine snow, sifting down and over, might easily suffocate any one buried in its depths.

Even as the sapling was crashing to the ground, he was leaping forward to lop off the branches—cutting each larger one about three inches from the trunk. Thus he had a single-pole ladder, up which one might easily climb. With a final slashing blow, he cut off the top, a full twenty-five feet from the other end. Then, using all his strength, he dragged the stout pole to the edge of the gorge near the hanging rope and, poking the heavier end over, worked it steadily down into the snow.

As he did so, he gazed anxiously downward. The white powder had sifted in on top of both boys, and only a faint hollow showed where they had gone down. There was no movement underneath, so far as he could see. The rope hung quietly, without a tremor. What was going on down below? What had happened? His heart was in his throat.

"I've got to go down and find 'em," he muttered. "I've *got* to. But how am I going to get them out? They're heavier than I."

He wedged the top of his "ladder" carefully in a crack in the stone edge. Then he began descending. The snow had mounted to his knees when, sev-eral feet upstream, a dead stick suddenly protruded through the surface and began a sort of circling motion, opening up a tube-like opening. This opening continually sought to fill in.

"Ahoy, Clement!" came faintly, in Walter's tones.

"Okeh, Walt!" cried Clement joyously.

"We're safe for the moment. Got a little air. We're in a pocket back under the gorge wall where the snow hasn't sifted in tight. Got your ladder?"

"I sent it down beside the rope," yelled Clement. "I was just coming down——"

"Stay up! Shift the ladder this way, if you can. Better draw it up and lower it again. Snow may come in on us any instant. Work fast!"

"Watch for it!" yelled Clement, as he joyously scrambled up.

It was a tremendous job to haul that ladder back. For a minute or so he thought he was not going to manage it. The little pegs were inclined slightly upward. They caught against the rock face. Moreover, the snow clung to the pole and held it down. Clement strained and tugged, seemingly in vain.

Suddenly an idea came. It took nerve, for it left those below without any chance of a way out. He jerked up the rope Walter had used. One end he flung over an overhanging oak bough. The other he attached to his pole. He edged the loop out on the branch until it hung away from the gorge edge. Then he put his full weight on the free end of the rope. For an instant nothing happened. Then he felt the snow yield its grip. Faster and faster the pole came upward. Clement barely avoided plunging into the depths himself. But he managed to swing to the rock in time.

Swiftly he jerked the pole free, swung it to the new position beside the still-moving dead stick, and lowered away. "Coming!" he yelled.

Suddenly he felt the pull of another hand on the pole, drawing the base in slightly. The ladder came to rest. He secured the top to prevent its swinging out. Then he waited anxiously. Almost at once there was evident a stirring and settling of the snow. The motion became more pronounced. Suddenly a head popped through, and Donald gazed up into Clement's anxious face. He drew a deep breath and then came on and toppled over on the ground.

"Whee!" he gasped. "She began caving in on us as I started. I held my breath, coming through that snow, until I thought I would burst. I——"

"Walter!" exclaimed Clement anxiously.

"Coming right after me," said Donald.

Clement stared down, more worried than he cared to let Donald see. Walter would have been under longer. If the snow had fully shut him in, he might be caught. Then Clement saw the snow was moving again. But more slowly and less perceptibly. Walter was not coming so fast.

All at once Clement could not stand it any longer. He swung over the cliff edge and started down. He was down to his waist, when he felt a hand grasp feebly at his ankle. Instantly he put his other foot lower, dropped down a peg, and groped for that hand. He caught it and pulled. He felt Walter heave himself slightly up, then begin to hang back.

Desperately Clement locked his legs around the pole and leaned far over, pawing a hole in the snow—down—down. Presently he felt his chum's fur cap. His groping fingers reached lower, opened a little channel to Walter's face, cleared his nostrils.

"The rope, Donald," he gasped. "We've got to haul him out."

Donald leaped for the hanging rope. But as he swung an end down to Clement, the latter felt Walter's sagging figure stiffen. His eyes opened and his grip strengthened. Aided by Clement's pulling arm, he took another step upward, and his face, oddly suffused, came into sight. He managed a faint smile of reassurance but made no effort to speak.

For a minute he rested, while Clement adjusted the rope under his shoulders. After that, with Donald pulling on the rope and Clement continuing to steady him, he gained the top and collapsed.

"It—caved in—on me," he gasped, "when Don started—up. I'll be—all right—in a minute."

"We'll camp here tonight," snapped Clement, with unusual positiveness for him. "Both of you have had enough."

Rather to conceal his own wrought-up condition, he picked up his ax and stepped off a little way to cut firewood. But he found it hard, now, to hit the mark. He haggled his cut; and once the ax hit glancingly and flew many feet away. Donald retrieved it and brought it back.

"You've done your daily good deed with a vengeance, Clem," he said, with a faint grin. "Must have been some job to handle that pole ladder all alone. Go over and rest. I'll do this. I'm all right." He gave his friend a shove. "Get out of here."

Clement obeyed and dropped beside Walter, while Donald went ahead and cut up a good supply of wood, besides clipping a lot of spruce branches to make springy mattresses on which to sleep. Then all joined in preparing supper, though the light was only beginning to fade. But they talked little until the meal had been eaten, a further supply of wood cut, and all arrangements made for the night's camp.

"You fellows were great," Donald exclaimed feelingly, when finally they were resting with backs to a boulder and facing a crackling fire of birch. "I don't like to think of the risk I put Walt to. I sure put my foot in it that time."

"Your foot, did you say, Don?" chuckled Walt. "It struck me you went in all over."

"I'll say," agreed Donald. "Hereafter, I'll take notice of warnings and keep out of trouble."

Clement and Walter exchanged smiling glances. Donald meant it, but it was as natural for him to fall into trouble as for a cat to lap milk.

"How did it feel, Don, to take a dive into fifteen or twenty feet of soft snow?" asked Clement.

"As easy as riding in an electric elevator," chuckled Don. "I just sank. No shock. Only it took so blamed long. Seemed hours. And I had as many thoughts, I suppose, as a drowning man might have. Fortunately I must have twisted somewhat in going down, for I broke into the edge of that shallow cave and knew I was safe."

Already darkness had stolen upon them. Flickering shadows, cast by the flames, seemed like moving creatures. Donald glanced about nervously. Clement, more of a woods lover, peered around or listened to the woods noises, interestedly. The wind talked in the spruce or rarer hemlock. An owl hooted dismally. Farther away a fox yapped; a wild cat screeched. Now and then standing dead timber snapped with loud reports and crashed. Stars came out and sparkled brilliantly in the clear, cold sky. The chill deepened. Walter added more fuel to the fire and suggested sleeping bags.

Then it came—a long-drawn-out plaintive, inexpressively wild ululation, that rasped the nerves and sent prickles coursing along one's spine.

"Sounds like The Black Shadow on the hunt," exclaimed Donald, leaping to his feet.

"Like but not exactly like; it's wilder," said Clement, glancing at Walter.

The latter looked thoughtful. "Good hearing, Clem!" he complimented. "Listen!"

Other howls came from back of the ridge. Presently several of the creatures were in full cry.

"Timber wolves," said Walter. "A small pack. Strange! They don't often run in these woods. Generally farther north. Bitter weather and poor hunting must have driven them down this way."

"Danger?" asked Donald. "We haven't a rifle with us."

"Hardly," said Walter. "This zero spell hasn't been long enough continued, and game is fairly abundant. Sorry to have those chaps get in to stir it up." He got to his feet. "I believe I'll chop a little more wood before turning in."

Donald and Clement exchanged glances, and the former stirred the fire into a brighter blaze.

In a short time Walter had added materially to the fuel supply. Then he began slipping into his sleeping bag. "Watch for a couple of hours, Clem," he directed. "Then call me. Don, try to get to sleep."

Walter himself fell asleep almost at once. There was something comforting to his companions in the ease and confidence with which he let himself go. But Don was wakeful, and he and Clement talked from time to time, listening, in between, to the howls of the pack that still hunted beyond the ridge. But finally even the wolves became silent, and Donald dozed off.

Then, suddenly, Clement was on his feet, and Walter and Donald were struggling out of their bags. Back along the trail they had made that afternoon, and not so far back at that, tumult had broken out. Vicious snarls and growls, the mouthings of two wolves in combat, broke the stillness. And then, clear and high, piercing through the harsh growlings, shrilled a long, whistling note.

"The Black Shadow!" yelled Donald.

"Raoul!" exclaimed Clement.

CHAPTER III
"So This Is the Boss?"

"QUICK!" SNAPPED WALTER. "HE may be in trouble. Stir the fire, Clem, and pile on fuel. I'll get my electric torch. Axes—that's it! Take two of the best burning brands, you two—the pitchy pine. Use 'em as torches. Wave 'em from time to time to keep up a blaze. Ready!" He lifted up his head and waited until a break came in the tumult of the fighting creatures. Then, deep and strong, he sent out the call, "Yo-heeeee—o!"

They listened. "Yo-heeeee-o!" flung back near-by cliffs, instantly. Then, in another subdued period of the wrangling voices, "Yo-heeee-o!" floated back to them, faint but very clear, from down the trail they had made early that afternoon.

"Let's go!" cried Walter, switching on his torch and starting rapidly back along the trail. His companions followed Indian file, axes on shoulders and waving their burning sticks. Ahead of them the tumult rose and fell, finally ending in yelps of pain and fear, and then ceasing as another sharp whistle cut the air.

The three sped stumblingly on. Now and again Walter gave voice to his call, and answering calls came with increasing clearness, though still some distance away. Presently he pointed to the snow bordering their trail. It was pitted with many doglike footprints. It was clear that the wolf pack had hit their trail and then, for some reason, had headed the other way.

They hurried on, a little breathlessly. "There!" yelped Donald tremulously, a few moments later. "To your left, Walt!"

Walter swung his torch ray. It illumined a great gray, skulking, doglike creature with rather pointed ears and a long snout. It's upper lip was drawn back, disclosing ugly fangs, and its red tongue hung out to one side. It snarled viciously. In the background the ray reflected from several pairs of greenish-amber round spots.

"Don't worry!" snapped Walter. "They won't bother us."

On they hurried again, waving their torches and showering sparks. Donald kept glancing about nervously, and was relieved to find the wolves did not appear to be following them. Then he looked ahead, and his eyes caught a movement near at hand to the right.

"Look out!" he shrieked. "There's one coming right at us from behind that bush. He's all bloody-mouthed. We've got to fight him off." He stuck his pine torch into the snow, and swung his ax from his shoulder.

"Steady, Don!" exclaimed Clement, with a little laugh in his voice. "It's all right. Here, Lupus!"

The animal loped over into the area of brighter light cast by the torches. He was large and somewhat wolflike. But he was black and not gray. Clearly a magnificent dog with wolf blood. As he came up, he gave an odd little yelp of delight and lunged straight at Clement. The latter fondled his great head.

"He's cut up a bit, Walt," cried Clement anxiously.

"Just slashed from his fight," said Walter, examining and petting him. "He'll be all right."

When Donald had taken his turn in greeting The Black Shadow, the three again hastened on. Lupus swung to heel back of Walter. Presently they rounded a bend and caught the flicker of firelight among some saplings not far ahead. As they drew nearer, a tall, dark, slender figure detached itself from the shadows and came towards them with that odd little limp they all remembered—the lifetime reminder of his terrible woods experience.

"Welcome in good time, my friends," he cried, arms outstretched. "Me, I am happy." He gripped each one's hands in turn, his dark eyes shining with pleasure.

"How came you on our trail, Raoul?" asked Walter, when greetings had been exchanged and the four had grouped themselves around a little camp fire, ignoring several gray wolves that sat on their haunches at a safe distance.

"Me, I'm coming from my home to join you at Camp Eighteen, Walt. I cut through this pass—like you, is it not?—making for Camp Seven. And today I cross a trail of three young men——"

"How did you know they were young?" broke in Donald.

Raoul smiled, showing his perfect white teeth. "The pressure in the snow, my friend. It is not deep enough for heavy men. Me, I say my friends are ahead and I will hasten and join them."

"How did you know——" began Donald, and stopped.

"Me—that you were ahead? Walt, he use old snowshoes that I remember. They have one leetle nick in one frame. I study the snow print and I know. I hasten, but the snow tell me the prints are some hours old; so I camp, saying, 'Me, I will reach you in the morning.'

"I sleep hard, I think. Then I wake, as Lupus, he snarl and charge. About six timber wolves, they are too near for comfort. Lupus, he fly at the leader. It is one grand fight. Only I whistle him back when that leader, he have enough. And Lupus does not like it, but he come. Lupus, he is far more good dog than bad wolf."

"But I see you had a rifle," exclaimed Donald. "Why not drive 'em off?"

"Me, I wake from sound sleep and know not how many wolves may be skulking in shadow." He shrugged his shoulders. "I see no tree about, big enough to climb. Me, I think I not start a fight unless necessary. But I do not understand. Me, I thought I read that trail. You must have been miles away. How come you to my aid?"

"We were delayed at Gorge Brook," explained Walter, "and so camped there."

"Because I was careless and toppled into trouble, as usual," added Donald. "You might as well hear the story." He told it.

Raoul looked very grave. "The woods, they are full of traps in winter," he said soberly.

Presently they all went along the trail to Gorge Brook and settled down to spend what was left of the night. Raoul insisted on taking first watch.

"Me, I do not think it necessary," he said. "This pack, from what we all saw, is small. And the wolves, they now have a puzzle in their heads. A big black wolf, he come and whip their leader. So he should be leader now. But he do not stay. He go to people they would like to eat. Is it not what you call a hard nut to splinter for the wolves?"

The wolves circled the camp all that night, but silently and at a distance. The place was ringed with their tracks by morning. They did not even make a threat of an attack, and with the morning light they skulked into the thickets and faded from sight.

"Me, I think we see the last of them for the present. But, Walt—" Raoul's manner became serious—"if winter, she stay hard as she threaten, and other wolves come in, there will be danger around the camps."

Walter nodded agreement but made no comment.

They were off to an early start, finding the snow packing and settling rapidly under the warmer sun. They made rapid progress. In late afternoon they broke from a thicket into a worn and rutty tote-road. Shortly new sounds came to their ears, coming from back in the woods—the "chunk—ka-chunk" of axes, the "z-z-z-inng" of rasping saws, and at intervals voices roaring, "*Timber-r-r-r!*" Walter's eyes brightened. He loved the woods life.

When they tramped into Camp Seven, they found only the cook and the cookee, or cook's assistant, to welcome them. But these outdid themselves in greeting them, and insisted on an impromptu meal, despite the fact that the regular evening dinner was but two hours away. They had partaken of this special refreshment and were outside when a motley gang of huskies of various nationalities came tramping in, led by the giant red-haired Pete Carmody, camp boss and most trusted field man of Big Jim Northrop's forces.

"If it ain't Big Jim's cockerel an' his friends!" roared Pete. "Welcome, me lads! Walt, ye're goin' t' be another Big Jim. I see it in y'r eyes an' frame."

"I'm proud to have you say it, Pete," returned Walter simply. "It's mighty good to see you and other friends of last summer. How about travel from here on, Pete? I want to hit Camp Eighteen ahead of my men."

"The railroad's blocked for days yet, me lad. Ye stay with me tonight. To-morrow, I give you a wood-sled with team an' driver an' a load of provisions for y'r camp. Ye can ride all the way; or to Camp Twelve an' tramp from there. Wish ye could stay an' see things hum around Seven, Walt. But you're right. Beat y'r men in, young boss."

"Any I know in the gang, Pete? I understand Dad had you help make the choice."

"I'm sending you Little John and Spareribs."

"Great! They alone ought to keep the gang contented. But it's sure hard on you, Pete, to lose 'em."

"Gives me an excuse t' come an' visit ye," grinned Pete, "t' sink me teeth in a square meal. Then, Walt, I'm sendin' ye Jean Dumas, Black Mike, Tod Owens, Ole Masson, and a dozen of men ye know. The rest is new, an' divil a bit do I know of 'em. Some thirty or thirty-five all told. An' ye'll use horses an' not tractors f'r skiddin'."

"Good enough!" said Walt. "Confidentially, Pete, Dad's had to hustle south on a long business trip. He telegraphed me to watch my step. What's up, do you know?"

"Divil a bit, lad," responded Pete seriously. "But if Big Jim says to watch y'r step, ye watch it, big boy. Me, I dunno. He may know of a trouble-maker in the gang. I sent 'im a list. Or it may be they is leaks. But there has been many accidents in camps this winter. You chaps has ears an' eyes. Use 'em."

The boys turned in early that night, wearied from their tramp and drugged with sleep because of the broken rest of the night before. Nevertheless, they were up with the first light and making ready for a prompt start. They found the big wood-sled already before the camp door, with two great draft horses attached. A young French Canadian, Paul LaJoie, was loading in provisions.

When all was ready, the driver and the four young chaps clambered aboard. There were no seats, so all perched, where they could get a fair degree of comfort, on boxes or cartons. Then farewells were uttered, and they started with a lurch.

"Watch your grip, you chaps," laughed Walter, with a grin at Raoul.

That good grip, Donald and Clement discovered at once, was vitally necessary. The trail through the new snow was only roughly broken open. Beneath the new fall were frozen ruts. Moreover, there appeared to be what might be termed permanent obstacles to smooth progress. Without warning the sled would strike stumps or small boulders with teeth-jarring jolts. One side of the sled or the other would tilt unexpectedly. Sometimes, too, there were sickening skids; or there were the beginnings of dangerous slides down-grade, checked by the simple expedient of running into soft snow or against a tree.

Even overturnings occurred. After the two less experienced travelers had been unceremoniously pitched head first into snowdrifts on several occasions, they learned to stand ready to jump when their driver uttered a warning cry. They even experimented with riding standing, as Walter and Raoul did, holding on to the stakes that rose from slots in the sides of the sled.

"Phe-ew!" puffed Donald, at one pause. "Every muscle in my body has been pulled, twisted, or jerked out of place."

"Limber you up for camp activities," chuckled Clement.

They passed camp after camp. At some, the men were busy digging out the railway; at others, all winter lumbering operations were in full swing. At intervals they were near enough to the cuttings to see the great trees crash down. Often they saw logs being moved along the trails.

It was at Camp Fourteen, the second camp beyond the end of the lumber railroad, that, in early afternoon, they met with their real adventure of the day. The tote-road, here, followed a lower level, at the foot of a long slope down which there were many signs of timbers having been skidded to rollways on the edge of a near-by stream. From the sounds that reached the travelers, lumbering operations were in full swing up the slope. Most of the skidway trails were icy and very slippery. Some of them had a very steep pitch just before they met the tote-road.

The wood-sled had rounded a bend in the rutty tote-road when a sharp yell of alarm came from the right. A lumberjack was skidding a great log down a narrow trail, using a horse team. He had just struck the steep section immediately above the road when the boys' team began to draw across his path. The great log, sliding forward on the slippery trail, was pressing dangerously close on the horses drawing it. The horses were speeding up.

Instantly all was confusion. The logger swung his team about to check the log, even as he yelled his warning. The team slipped and fell. The end of the log clipped a tree, broke loose, and catapulted down like a battering ram in action.

The boys' driver first started to rein in his team, but the horses slipped on a glare spot, and the sled slid on. Then, too late, young Paul whipped up, trying to pull out ahead of the timber. Instantly he saw he could not make it.

"Jump!" he screamed, lunging off headlong.

The four boys strove to follow his example, just as the great log came crashing in. It hit the vehicle a tremendous buffet just back of the mid-section, shoving the sled viciously around, upsetting the horses, and playing havoc with the load of provisions. Meanwhile all the boys, except Clement, were hurtling through the air to land safely in the snow.

Clement, unfortunately, was riding in such a position that the log appeared to be heading directly at him. He hesitated, fearing he might land directly in the path of the monster. So he leaped only at the last instant. By chance, a skidding swing of the great timber, as it glanced away from the sled under the impact, carried its great bole directly under him. He landed squarely astride. Instinctively his hands gripped it desperately, and he rode it through its final slide until it brought up square against a standing tree. At that he shot off, took two or three involuntary somersaults and, to his own utter astonishment and that of his chums, ended the last revolution by landing waveringly on his feet.

"Bully boy, Clem!" yelled Donald, picking himself out of a drift and digging the snow out of his ears and neck. "Regular broncho riding stunt! If you can stick to a log like that, Walt will train you to handle ornery logs in the spring drive."

Clement was more than a little white, and he still wore a dazed expression, but he came back gamely. "Always knew I could do circus stunts," he chuckled. "Only, next time, give a fellow fair warning, won't you, and supply saddle and bridle—and spurs, particularly spurs. They would help one to stick on better."

They looked then for Walter. They found him sitting on the head of one of their horses, while Raoul held down the other. Thus the animals were kept quiet until their harness could be disentangled. Things indeed were in considerable of a mess. The sled was badly smashed, and several cases of provisions had been broken open. Some of the material was destroyed.

An hour was lost while word was sent to the camp boss, another sled secured, and the usable provisions were transferred. Then they were off again, and Walter kept them traveling after the sun had set and darkness was fast blotting out the ruts of the tote-road. In fact, a new moon was shining brightly over the long, low structure of the Men's Camp when they swung into Camp Eighteen. Progress had been exceptionally slow after leaving Camp Seventeen, for from there on the road had not been broken open. The drifts were many and deep, and more than once they had had to dig their way through. The whole party, as well as the horses, were exhausted.

Wearily they unhitched the team and put the horses up in the stables. Then they had still more digging before them in order to get into the small log hut Walter intended to use for his own party. After that wood had to be secured for fuel and a fire started to raise the icy temperature to a point of safety. Then, a hurried meal, and they toppled into their bunks to sleep, dead to the world, until the sun was high in the heavens the next morning.

But morning brought no relief from toil for any of the five. Walter was anxious to have the main camps open and heated before the camp force should arrive in late afternoon. So there were more deep drifts to be broken open, paths to be cleared, and great fires to be started and tended. Provisions had to be unloaded and things made ready for rapid work by Little John and Spareribs in getting an evening meal for a force that would be sure to be ravenously hungry.

"I want to see things started right," said Walter. "It means a lot in handling a big gang."

Clement studied his friend thoughtfully. Walter was far more serious than usual. It was clear that he was already feeling the strain of the responsibility that was to rest on his young shoulders. Yet Clement had no fear but that he would carry successfully whatever load came upon him.

It was around four in the afternoon when, far down the trail, the little group heard voices and even the sharp crack of whips as the heavy-laden sleds came on. The woodsmen were shouting at one another, roaring with laughter, and now and then breaking into some rollicking lumberman's song, the men making the air ring with the chorus.

Presently the first team hove in sight around a bend—four horses, drawing a heavy sled carrying a dozen men. Behind came other teams, a half dozen, laden with men and camp equipment. The men whooped at sight of the camp buildings, and Walter, stepping forward, waved his arms and cried a greeting.

The lead team came to a halt before the Men's Camp, with the others drawing up behind. From the foremost sled an elephantine figure rolled and clambered down, wavered unsteadily for a moment on the slippery footing, then waddled forward towards Walter with great arms outstretched.

"*By gar!*" he yelled, in high falsetto. "If it be'nt th' leetle boss—Big Jim's son." His great paw gripped Walter's hands. Then he pushed the youngster back and stared. "Me, I'm happee to be here. *Un homme* grown! Me, I put more flesh on that strong frame! Wait till ye eat what Little John cooks for one leetle week."

"Remember, you old rascal," chuckled Walter, his face shining with pleasure, "that I've hard work to do. Don't tempt me to become a man mountain like you."

Little John chuckled, and his enormous masses of flesh quivered like jelly. Then his eyes sought the cook's shed. "By gar! Me, I get a real meal. Spareribs, get ze fire hot or I make mincemeat of ye, ye leetle midge."

From behind the giant appeared the short and skeleton-like cookee. Yet his hand grip was like iron as he greeted his young boss, with no word, yet with a swift, loyal glance from dark eyes. Then, swinging on his immediate superior, he glared hotly, growling in an unexpectedly deep voice, "*Pig!* How you expect me to work, after you've rolled me flatter'n one of yore own pancakes every time we hit a stump? Me, I'll yet fry yuh in yore own fat."

"*By gar!*" shrieked Little John. "Ye bit o' nothin'! *Cochon!* She dare mak' fun of mine pancakes." He aimed a tremendous buffet at his diminutive assistant, missing his mark as Spareribs dodged expertly. The momentum of the blow destroyed his own balance, and he crashed heavily with a loud "Umph!" of expelled breath.

Roaring with laughter, two lumberjacks strained and pulled and finally got him on his feet, and he waddled off shrieking threats at Spareribs. But the threats disturbed no one. Cook and cookee were known to be devoted friends.

By now the other men were crowding forward. In the first ranks were many lumberjacks whom Walter knew, including Jean and Black Mike. There the greeting was warm and hearty and tinged with a certain respect. But back of them came more than a dozen men, strangers all, now engaged for the first time to work in Big Jim's camps. These men gazed curiously, and evidently with mingled feelings, at the slender young chap who stepped forward to greet them. They were powerful and husky men, all of them, some young, some of middle age with the scars of their dangerous trade upon them. Used to fighting camp bosses who could lick them in a rough and tumble, surprise and amusement and a certain contempt shone in expressive faces.

"So this is the boss?" queried one, almost sarcastically, as Walter stepped forward to meet them. He was a powerful young man, red of hair and with merry devils of mischief in his brown eyes. "When did the school teacher let you out, eh?"

He stepped forward with an insolent air and held out his hand. As Walter took it, his great fingers clinched for a crushing grip. But Walter's own hand shifted before it was too late, finding the pressure point he sought. He gripped. Moisture broke out on the young man's forehead, his lips tightened with pain as he strove to meet that unexpected vise-like hold.

For an instant they stood thus, until all power had gone from the stranger's fingers. Then Walter dropped the other's hand. "Your name?" he inquired quietly.

"Terry Connors," answered the other shortly, yet now with a vague respect.

Walter turned to the others and, one by one, exchanged a word or so and asked names. The incident with Terry had not missed their shrewd eyes. They answered courteously enough. But as they picked up their turkeys and turned to go up to the Men's Camp, a hulking, sandy-haired giant with cold bluish eyes snarled to a companion. "That a boss? Huh! I c'n break him across my knee with one hand. Terry, I'm thinkin' we've struck clover, where we c'n take it easy."

There was a snarl of anger back of Walter, and Black Mike shoved by, his fists clenched, his eyes hot with anger. The young boss caught him and sent him spinning aside.

"This is my affair, Black Mike," he said quietly.

CHAPTER IV
The Spirit Moose Again

A SUDDEN HUSH HAD fallen on the crowd. The men who knew Walter moved close up behind him. The strangers remained bunched, facing him. Yet it was evident at a glance that not all these newcomers were backing the giant lumberjack.

Walter's color had faded slightly, but his eyes were keen and cold. There was no slightest sign of flinching in manner or voice.

"Men," he ordered quietly, "put up your dunnage and then get busy. All provisions must be stored in the cook's storehouse. All tools will go into the toolhouse. Jean, you supervise that. Here's the key." He tossed it to him. "Other equipment will be stored in the covered way between the Men's Camp and the Mess Camp. You men who are stablemen, get the horses under cover and rub 'em down. Some are overheated, I notice. Then feed and water 'em. That——"

"Oh, come!" growled the sandy-haired giant. "All this can wait until morning, except for the horses. We've had a hard trip and a light lunch. We need rest and food. These things can be done in the morning, *Boss*." The last word was uttered with a sneer.

"Your name's Bart Johannes, isn't it?" inquired Walter steadily.

"That'll do for my handle," responded the giant truculently.

"Meaning," inquired Walter slowly and pointedly, "that you've gone by other names as well?"

"What's that to you?" snarled Bart viciously, swinging a step forward.

"Perhaps little, perhaps much," smiled Walter. Suddenly his jaw stiffened and his voice pounded: "Listen, Johannes! Either you obey orders at once and without further insolence, or you start backtracking out of camp this minute. Make up your mind. Which is it to be? *Quick!*"

Johannes started to spring forward, but one of his own crowd reached out an arm to jerk him back. The man muttered in his ear. Johannes glared furiously at the young boss. Yet he yielded, not wholly because of the advice he evidently had received, but because he could not but sense that the young man had strong support.

"All right," he snarled savagely and stamped away to grab his turkey from the sled. But he growled, "For this time," as he went.

"Gee!" exclaimed Donald when Walter had made his assignments and for a moment the four young chaps were alone. "You were great, Walt. I wouldn't have missed that first clash for a year's growth."

"I would have missed it gladly," returned Walter soberly. "It's bad to clash at the first moment, but it had to be." Suddenly he grinned ever so slightly at Clement. "Here's where I begin to watch my step."

"And we'll be watching with you," declared Clement earnestly. "At least, Walt, as I studied their faces, it seemed to me that all the old men and fully half of the new were with you. That ought to hold things."

"I'm more concerned in having everything go smoothly than in holding things," said Walter. "Two or three hostile men are like yeast, in a gang like this. They leaven the whole lump. And don't forget, Clem, though these men are friendly in large measure, they're easily disgruntled under the terrifically hard work and the restrictions of a lumber camp. At any time a few may rally around trouble-makers, and a blow-up follows."

"Why not toss the fellow out on his ear right now?" demanded Donald.

"I think," said Walter slowly, "that Johannes is a firebrand. Of course, he may only be getting off on the wrong foot; but he may be doing this intentionally. I'd like, even at the cost of harboring trouble in our midst, to keep him until I know."

Two hours later Little John whaled a large metal triangle, hanging outside the cook shack, with a great maul, swung by his mighty arm. In response to the clangor the men trooped into the Mess Camp and ranged themselves at the long table that extended down the center, almost the length of the building. Speech was at a minimum for a time, but there were not lacking many sounds of clinking dishes and the rattle of knives, forks, and spoons, as the heaped dishes of beans and pork and bread and gingerbread melted away, and great buckets of strong tea were emptied into giant tin cups.

Walter sat with his friends at the far end of the long table. He appeared at ease and ate heartily. He seemed to send only casual glances down the board, yet he was alertly sizing up the gang which, for many weeks, he would command. He noted, not without interest, that fully half the new men had found places among the old Northrop lumberjacks. The few newcomers who clung together were clustered around young Terry and Johannes at the other end of the table. Here was some low-muttered interchange of comment, despite the heavy work of stoking the human engines.

Gradually one man after another leaned back emitting sighs of repletion and satisfaction. Several flung words of approval at Little John, as the latter waddled about the room, watchful of last-minute needs and shrieking high-pitched orders at Spareribs. Pipes came out, the air thickened, and conversation mounted noisily. In the rough badinage, more than one remark was hurled at Walter or his companions. But they took the flings handily and tossed back keen and humorous retorts.

Raoul, going out on some errand, came back presently, tagged by The Black Shadow. The men gazed at the great beast with interest. The adventures of this dog and his master had already taken on a sort of legendary character. The dog turned away from his master and began circling the table, accepting the advances of the lumberjacks in dignified fashion. In fact, Lupus's dignity seldom left him, save when he romped with his master or with Clement, for whom he had a special fondness.

"If only Skipper were here!" murmured Donald longingly. He was utterly devoted to the lively young fox terrier that had been his constant companion—in and out of all escapades—during the two previous trips he had taken into the big woods. "Lupus would like him here, too."

"I feared we might have some snow tramping to do," said Walter, "in getting out here. That's why I advised you to leave him home. We would have lost him that first blizzardy day in the loose, drifting snow. He could never have tagged after us. But now you might have him shipped up."

"I'll write tonight," exclaimed Donald eagerly, "so the letter can go out by the first messenger."

Meanwhile Lupus was continuing his slow progress, stopping now and then to accept some choice morsel a man offered him, but only after a glance back to his master to be sure it was permitted. Finally he rounded the end of the table and stopped beside Johannes.

"Get out of here, you!" snarled the man viciously, kicking out at the same time with his great booted foot.

The Black Shadow did not retreat; he crouched, his eyes red, his lips drawn back from his fangs. In an instant more he would have hurled himself at the throat of the man. But Raoul's command, "Here, Lupus!" snapped sharply. The dog responded, withdrawing slowly, but with a threat in each movement and backward glance.

"You attack that dog," said Raoul quietly, but with a peculiar steely quality in his tones, "and it will be your last minute on this earth. Me, I'm telling you. He know what you are."

"And I'm warning you I'll make dead meat of him if he makes a move," Johannes flung back with a string of oaths.

"You injure that dog," flared Black Mike unexpectedly, "and I beat you to a pulp. Me, I can do it."

Johannes had sprung to his feet, and Walter was up too, fearing a physical clash. Then, muttering abuse, the former swung about and stormed out of the camp, followed by some of his following. The door crashed on their going. A new freedom seemed to settle on those that were left; the men seemed happier and more gay.

A couple of hours later, with the camp fast settling to quiet for the night, Walter and his friends tramped through the bitter night back to their own quarters. The northern sky glittered and shimmered with dancing stringers of greenish gold and rose—a gorgeous northern lights display.

"Leesen!" exclaimed Raoul suddenly, as the boys stood enjoying the glorious sight. He held up his hand.

At once they caught it—a long-drawn, plaintive howl. Beside them The Black Shadow stiffened. He dropped to his haunches, lifted his nose, and sent out an answering eerie howl. Far away other howls succeeded. And after a little, as the boys still listened, they heard the yelps and howls of a hunting pack in full cry.

"Me, I'm thinking it will be the same pack," said Raoul, answering the others' unspoken thought. "The pack is working this way and it is growing, my friends. Camp Eighteen, it is the spearpoint in our line of camps, pushing ahead of all others into the deep woods. We watch, you and I. All sights point to a bitter winter. Me, I read them in the trees and in the animals. That pack may threaten—our teams, men caught far out alone. There is danger in that pack." His tone held a thread of amusement, rare in him. "It have no Little John to get its meals."

"We will watch," agreed Walter. "If danger threatens, certain men on the outposts must go armed."

"And, Lupus," went on Raoul, "for the present you do not hunt at night. Me, I say it. Much you love me; but the call of the wild, it is very strong, and already you have whipped that pack leader."

"Johannes will have it in for Lupus," said Walter soberly.

"Me, I know it," answered Raoul. "That man, Walt, we all fight when the time comes."

With the first dawn the camp force was stirring. The sun was still below the horizon when the triangle clanged its clarion call to another good meal. When that was stowed away, Walter's orders came thick and fast as he strove to organize his forces and set his camp in action.

It had already been decided that Clement was to handle the field and camp record books. So he took these at once and began to try to master them, listing questions, as he went along, that Walter would answer when he had time.

Donald, for the time being, was to be in charge of the Wanigan Camp, the small structure which housed the personal stores which lumberjacks wish to purchase. These included sweaters, mittens, moccasins, larrigans, leggings, boots, flannel underwear, pipes, and tobacco. The camp was open only at a few stated hours. Thus Donald was left free to act as Walter's messenger or to assist him in other ways.

Raoul, a trained timber cruiser and lumber expert, despite his youth, was to act as Walter's assistant in marking out "cuts" and laying out the work of the felling crews.

For the first two days Walter kept practically all his men at the task of opening up tote-roads, runways, trails, and rollways. All these had been cleared out the summer before but now lay deeply buried under the snow. Often only a woodsman's instinct could locate these under the unbroken white blanket.

During this period Walter was sizing up the men and questioning them, as a basis for assigning them to duty as fellers, sawyers, swampers, and skidders and stablemen. Also he had to see that several of the sleds that had brought in loads were started back to the camps to which they belonged. In addition, he directed the checking and listing of all equipment and the issuing of tools to the men.

Late on the second afternoon, Walter at last found time to take Raoul and start off on a reconnaissance over the camp limits, with a view to refreshing his mind as to the stands of timber and formulating plans for starting cutting. They took Lupus, and Walter carried his rifle.

They tramped rapidly out the trail that led to the fire tower where they had been on guard the year previous. Then they swung left through unbroken forest, heading around towards the camp in a great circle. Now and then Walter stopped to make notations of the tract on maps which he always kept with him in the field.

They were well on their way around and within two miles of camp when they approached a low ridge beyond which lay a low swampy area of alder thickets and moosewood. Here The Black Shadow began to show considerable excitement and a tendency to shoot away as if on some trail. He returned to Raoul with very evident reluctance when his master called him.

"Wolves?" queried Walter.

"Me, I think not," responded Raoul. "He show no anger. Game of some kind, big game—perhaps a bear that do not hole up for some reason."

"Suppose we take a look about," said Walter. "There's time before dark."

"From the top of that ridge we take a view over the lowlands," suggested Raoul.

At Walter's nod of agreement, he took the lead and swung off and up the slope. The great wolf dog, fairly quivering with eagerness, kept obediently at his master's heels. Swiftly but silently they moved up the flat slope, making use of cover where possible, and searching the surrounding area with the utmost care. They topped the ridge without sighting any game and began to descend the farther slope, heading towards the crest of a tiny cliff, whence there was an abrupt drop to the lowland level.

With every step, now, Lupus's excitement increased. But the intelligent beast perfectly understood that his master was stalking the creature he had scented and that he must not give tongue to any call. He moved a little ahead of Raoul and headed of his own accord towards the point the two young men had already chosen. All approached the edge of the drop with the utmost caution, finally dropping to their knees and crawling the last few feet.

Raoul was the first to carefully lift his head and peer over. Almost at once he drew it slowly back. His eyes were shining as he motioned Walter to follow his example. Already Walter had sensed in general what he should see. Inch by inch, with no sudden motion that would attract a wild animal's attention, he stretched forward and peered outward and down. Then he barely suppressed a sharp movement of surprise and delight.

Almost at the foot of the cliff, some fifty feet below, a large space among young saplings had been trampled down. In this space stood or lay several enormous ungainly brownish-gray creatures with very coarse hair, long heads, prehensile lips. Three had thick branching antlers.

"A moose yard!" Walter gasped to himself. He had expected a deer yard. Then he started again as he got a better view of the largest and oldest of the three bulls. He was an enormous fellow with perfectly tremendous antlers—only once had he seen so wonderful a moose. For a moment more he stared down, then softly drew back. With Raoul, he retired some distance before he dared speak.

"It *is*!" he murmured then. "It's the Spirit Moose. I'd know that chap's head anywhere. Isn't it great, having him travel up this way! If only Lupus doesn't hunt that band out of here!"

"Him, I can make understand," said Raoul. "But me, I think there are other dangers, Walt. The wolf pack, and perhaps our men! Some one may poach. And anyhow, when felling begins, the noise may scare them off. But for those reasons they might stay all winter."

"Wouldn't it be great, Raoul—" Walter's eyes shone at the thought—"if we could tame that fellow and use him as a camp mascot!"

"Me, I've heard of its being done," said Raoul. "A little grain or hay, if this bitter weather holds, and he may be brought nearer the camp. We will try. I——" He stopped, clutched his companion's arm and pointed far to the right.

Two figures were stealing through the bushes, evidently on some trail of a moose. They were lumberjacks, clearly, and one carried a rifle. The men clearly had not, as yet, spotted the yard, but their course would soon bring them into view of it.

"Me, I think poaching have begun," said Raoul.

"I'll stop it *before* it begins," snapped Walter.

"Is it wise, my friend?" queried Raoul. "You run into danger and perhaps do not stop them. You have no authority."

"Oh, but I have," laughed Walter softly. He felt in his pocket and pulled out a metal badge which he attached to his coat. "Here's my evidence of my appointment as deputy forest ranger. Remember, I served last year? The appointment has never been canceled. I found the badge when I was packing and stuck it in my bag. Remember, Raoul, in this state, the forest ranger has the powers of a game warden."

"It may work," conceded Raoul. "But watch your step! Me, I think we better take them by surprise. Huh?"

Walter nodded and waved Raoul into the lead. The young French Canadian ordered The Black Shadow to heel and started off. A true woodsman, he moved swiftly, instinctively choosing an easy course and taking advantage of every bit of cover should the two stalkers glance back. He moved in the approximate arc of a circle, aiming to get behind them.

As they proceeded, they had many glimpses of the two lumberjacks. Presently they saw the man in the lead come to a sharp halt and motion excitedly to his companion. Clearly the yard had been spotted, perhaps the giant moose. The men crouched and began an approach with the utmost caution. Behind them, Walter and Raoul closed up the gap as fast as possible. Finally they were within fifty paces.

Walter now watched like a hawk as the men ahead halted and one raised his rifle. A cry was in the young deputy's throat. But the man lowered his rifle and shifted again. Satisfied, he kneeled, lifted his weapon, and took aim.

"*Stop!*" yelled Walter harshly.

The man started nervously and leaped to his feet. Both woodsmen swung around. And Walter found himself staring into the faces of young Terry and of Johannes. The former held the rifle. Seeing who had held him up, he relaxed and grinned.

"Gorry, Boss!" he exclaimed. "You sure gave me a start. But keep quiet a minute. I got a bead on the giant of all moose. I——"

"Which you're not going to shoot, Terry."

"And why not?" demanded the red-head in all seriousness. "Just think how some moose steaks would taste, cooked by Little John."

"You're not shooting any moose, today or any day, for the present," insisted Walter.

"Who's stopping me?" grinned Terry, yet with his eyes sparking. "You're not going to shoot *me*, are you, if I try?"

"I'll see that the young cockerel doesn't," growled Johannes. "Here, gimme that rifle." He snatched it from his companion's hands and swung towards the yard.

Walter sprang forward. But Raoul made a sign to the watchful Lupus. The Black Shadow shot by Walter as if fired from a cannon crashing against Johannes. The man fell headlong, his rifle flying from his hands. And before he could recover from his astonishment and shock, the wolf dog stood over him, his teeth at the man's throat.

"Take him off!" snarled Johannes, the color draining from his face.

Walter cast a rather reproachful glance at Raoul. "This was my job, my friend," he said softly. Then he stepped forward and snatched up the rifle from the snow. "Back, Lupus!" he ordered quietly. As the dog drew away a few steps, still watchful, Walter added, "Get up!"

Johannes struggled shakily to his feet. "Hang you!" he muttered. "Can't you boss your own affairs. Have to call on a dog to help."

"That is false," put in Raoul, "and me, I think you know it. I set Lupus on you. Your boss did not like it. He was right."

"Whose is this rifle?" demanded Walter. "It was not reported when I listed all weapons in camp."

"Mine," growled Johannes, "and I'll report it or not, as I please. You little whippersnapper, you've no right to hold me up. I'll shoot——" He stopped, his eyes widening as their gaze fastened on the nickel shield on Walter's coat. His manner changed. "But you won't make trouble for me, Boss? Over the game laws? No one obeys them here in deep woods."

"They will be obeyed in my camp," said Walter coldly. "I'll lock this gun up until you leave our employ. Why are you two not at work? You were supposed to be clearing trails."

Johannes flushed and growled something under his breath. Terry's merry, teasing eyes sparkled. "Forget it this time, Boss! We were far out this way when we hit a moose trail. Just couldn't resist. And it was near the end of the day, anyhow."

"I'll dock both of you for lost time," declared Walter. "If there is more trouble, out you go. Get back on your jobs."

He let the men precede him, then followed with Raoul and The Black Shadow. But gradually the latter group dropped farther behind.

"Terry is not a bad sort," said Walter. "I don't see what he finds in Johannes."

"Me, I think he'll soon get bad in that company," returned Raoul.

They tramped on in silence in the fading light. Suddenly Raoul, first making sure that the lumberjacks were out of sight, swung sharply to one side. He pointed down in the snow. Long tracks appeared in the surface.

"Skis!" snapped Walter thoughtfully. "And going away from camp. What does this mean? Where was that person headed? Tomorrow we trail him. It is getting too dark now. Wait, Raoul, you explore to the left and I to the right and come back to this point. There may be other trails."

Raoul nodded and swung swiftly away. Walter sped to the right. Presently he found what he sought and sent a soft call after his companion. When Raoul joined him, he pointed at his feet. "The skier came in this way. Let us follow his 'in' trail."

At full speed they followed on the ski trail. In the course of a half mile, and not far from the cleared trails, the ski tracks joined with snowshoe tracks.

"So," said Walter, "a messenger from somewhere else comes in to talk with Johannes and Terry. The plot thickens. Why did he come and from where?"

"Me, I read more in these signs," said Raoul. "The ski-runner met only Johannes here. Those snowshoe tracks, they sink deep. Very heavy man. Also, the tracks all alike. Terry, he not here. Wait. I circle about. Me, I am interested."

Again Raoul circled off. He was gone some time, but when he came back his eyes showed excitement.

"Me, I read it this way," he said. "Johannes, he slip away and meet the ski-runner. Terry, he see him go and take another trail. Perhaps he spy on Johannes. Who knows? Later he overtakes him and they go on together."

"Now, what do we make of that!" muttered Walter.

CHAPTER V
"Timber-r-r-r!"

WALTER AND RAOUL DISCUSSED the matter as they hastened campwards. They came to no conclusion, save that it was important to find whence the ski-runner had come. That might be from one of their own camps or from those of Oddie, whose timberlands adjoined the Northrop holdings. But that something was afoot and trouble brewing neither boy doubted.

"I feel," said Walter, "that Dad believes a trouble-maker is at work. Perhaps he suspects someone who is in our crew, and his 'Watch your step' was a general warning to be on guard. For some reason, he might have thought it would handicap me in a way to let me know the particular person he suspected. I might overlook others."

"Me, I believe you are right," agreed Raoul.

"I must start the felling of timber tomorrow," went on Walter, "so I'll have you trail that ski-runner. Clement can go with you."

"We will do our best," promised Raoul. "But you watch that Terry, in addition to Johannes."

"I'll do that," agreed Walter.

But, after all, Raoul did not trail the ski-runner. He woke in the early morning to find the air thick with flying snow. Evidently it had been snowing for several hours, for a three-inch coverlid of white crystals overlay the previous falls. All snow tracks had disappeared.

Still, Raoul had an errand away from camp that morning. He departed with a bagful of grain and tidbits, such as he thought might tempt a moose's palate. These he scattered from the edge of the moose yard towards the camp, as a first step in enticing the moose in that direction.

"The only thing to do about that runner," said Walter, when Raoul reported back, "is to add Clement and Don to those on guard. That will make four of us constantly watching for signs of any stranger coming in. I'd like to inquire if any man was missing yesterday from our camps down the line, but I think it unwise to do so just yet."

A light snow being no handicap to lumbering operations, field work really began that morning. The whole force tramped out as soon as the morning meal was over. Even Little John waddled along in company with Spareribs, to see the work start. It was the beginning of the winter cut in a new camp, and as such Big Jim Northrop always allowed a little ceremony.

"The boss, he fells the first timber," cried Black Mike, when all stopped at the edge of the tract where cutting was to begin. Others echoed the suggestion enthusiastically. Only Johannes sneered.

"How about a contest, Black Mike, you and I?" laughed Walter.

Several of the woodsmen exclaimed at the idea. They remembered, a few of them, a contest in Camp Seven the summer before, when Black Mike, secure in his tremendous strength and skill, had loafed in a chopping contest and lost to Walter.

Black Mike was clearly pleased. He started to agree; then he shook his head. "You might lick me," he acknowledged. "But for me to win, it might not be fair. Me, I have been cutting all winter in other camps; the boss, not until now. Me, I wait until you get your hand in."

"Good sport, Black Mike!" cried Clement impulsively.

Black Mike reddened with pleasure. "The boss, he taught me," he answered simply. Then he grinned. "Boss, you choose a timber, say where you will lay it down, and put it there."

Walter chuckled. "Putting me to the test, I see. All right! I'm game." He glanced about him. The area was one of hard woods, mainly excellent yellow birch. Finally he selected a tree of about eighteen inches in diameter at the butt. It was slightly twisted some thirty feet up and ever so slightly inclined. A real test! "I'll take this one," he said.

He stepped back and studied the great bole of the tree; then he considered the wind and the neighboring trees. Finally he made a long mark in the snow. "She'll do the least damage to other timber if she falls here," he said. "Here goes!"

Swiftly his ax rose, swung in a gleaming arc, and, with a solid "chunk," bit deep into the birch. He pulled the blade free, and swung again. Then, steadily, he cut his notch, the great chips sailing out over the snow while the ax talked. "Chunk—ka-chunk—ka-chunk!"

When halfway through, he studied his tree again, then opened up his notch slightly on one side and again deepened it. A faint crackle of straining fibers sounded. The top trembled perceptibly. He stepped around the bole for the under-cut. The tree bowed ever so slightly. Fibers cracked like rifle shots. A shiver ran along the entire trunk.

"*Timber-r-r-r-r!*" he yelled in his clear, carrying voice.

He brought his blade down, sharp and clean. The crackling increased. The great tree dipped low. Then it crashed with ever increasing speed. There were a swishing roar and a heavy thud. Snow showered in every direction, while from the stump wood splinters hurtled backward. The first fell had been made.

A roar went up from the men. The mark that Walter had drawn in the snow had been wholly covered. He had made good. Johannes, however, gave a snort of disgust and said something sneeringly to Terry. Yet there was unwilling respect in the glance he sent towards his superior.

Meanwhile Walter was already clipping off the branches of the tree with swift, well-placed blows, lopping off the crown, and marking the points where the timber must be cross-cut into commercial lengths.

"You, Black Mike," he called, "come and saw with me."

Grinning broadly, Black Mike ran forward, leaped the timber, and gripped one of the upright handles of the great cross-cut saw which Walter had already set at the first mark.

"Ready! *Go!!*" he roared.

Instantly the saw began to talk. "Z-zing—z-zing-ng—z-zing!" The speed mounted. Yellow dust spouted, spewed out by the rakers. The two sawyers lunged and thrust and pulled—soon at astounding speed—while the crew of woodsmen roared and whooped encouragement. Black Mike grinned broadly. He was playing his little joke on his boss to somewhat balance his previous consideration. He was striving to make his partner either cry "Enough" or simply keep his hand on the handle while he himself did the work.

But Walter, though his color rose and perspiration broke out on his forehead, kept pace with Black Mike's speed. The latter's great back and shoulder muscles flowed smooth as silk. His tremendous strength was evident. But Walter always kept himself in athletic trim. And now, though his breath came fast, he stuck to his task, shoving and pulling hard. And suddenly, with a sharp report, the cut was complete.

"Next," gasped Walter, picking up the saw, running to the second mark and setting the blade against it. Black Mike was but a second behind him. Again the "z-zing—z-zing" filled the air and the sawdust spouted. But that instant spent in changing had given Walter his second wind. He stuck gamely to the end. And at that end each eyed the other with respect and approval.

"You'd break me, Black Mike," chuckled Walter, "if I had to work opposite you all day. What next, men?"

"A felling contest," Jean suggested, "between Little John and Spareribs!"

The crew whooped with delight.

"Me waste time with that leetle midge?" Arms akimbo, Little John brought his big blue eyes to bear on the cookee. "Give me some-un my size. That no 'count leetle shrimp. *Bah!*"

"No circus around here to loan a fat man," chuckled Jean. "You willing to tackle that elephant, Spareribs?"

Spareribs spat disgustedly. In his surprisingly deep voice he roared, "Me, I show who chops the firewood in that shebang." He waved a hand towards camp. "Here's two trees." He laid his hands on two birches of about equal size. "Take y'r choice, ye man mountain. I'll run the fat off'n ye."

Little John tapped a tree. "*By gar!*" he squealed. "She insult me, that leetle speck o' nothin'. Me, I show heem. With two strokes I fell thees tree. Hunh?"

"Ready!" cried Jean. "Get set! *Go!!*"

Spareribs swung a lightning stroke at his timber. Little John poised his ax dramatically, gave a tremendous swing, and aimed a smashing blow at his own tree. But he swung so mightily that he destroyed his own balance. Moreover, his footing on the slippery snow was none too secure. His feet flew from under him, and his ax, glancing from the tree, was wrenched from his grip and flew through the air straight towards Spareribs. The latter dodged, the ax whistling by his ear and clipping into the bark of his tree.

Little John, sitting up with the breath knocked from him, stared in horror as the ax flew at his cookee. Then he grinned as if perfectly satisfied. "By gar!" he cried. "She no count. We start again—is it not so, nitwit?"

"He tried to tomahawk me," roared Spareribs, with pretended fury. "Ye are witnesses that he would brain me with an ax. Now ye will believe how he treats me in the cook shack. Whales me with sticks of firewood, throws pots an' pans at me." He picked up the ax and carried it back to the seated Little John. With it he passed over a piece of cord. "Ye murderin', threatenin' blowhard! Tie the ax to y'r arm an' see if ye c'n keep holt of it. Get up, ye lazy porpoise, an' get set!"

The winded Little John was helped to his feet by woodsmen who were themselves weak from laughter. Again the word was given and the contest begun. But now Little John appeared timid. That fall had been too terrific to bear the chance of repetition. He swung lightly.

Spareribs surprised all with powerful, well-placed blows—for a minute or so. Then he let up to glare at his superior. "Get going, ye boastin' Humpty Dumpty!" he roared.

He rested on his ax for a half minute. Then he chopped rapidly for a few strokes and rested again. Meanwhile Little John belabored his own tree and gradually haggled out the semblance of a notch. So Spareribs tolled him on, while tears of laughter rolled down the cheeks of the crew.

Wholly unexpectedly, Little John began to swing his ax. The blade cut deep and true. Great chips sailed away into the underbrush. And instantly Spareribs was in tense action also. The two ax blades rang almost as one. The race tightened. The men sprang around for the reverse cut. Tremblings ran up the boles at almost the same instant.

"*Timber-r-r-r-r!*" yelled the two men in chorus.

The trees bowed—crashed. By a split second Spareribs' tree hit first. And instantly the little man was on its trunk, preening himself and yelling, "Me, I win. The saw, now!"

"By gar, *no!*" piped Little John. "Me handle a saw with that speck o' dust? Me, I got a real meal to cook. Come on, ye runt!" He made a derisive gesture in the general direction of the cookee. "She think she c'n chop. Let heem try it on the firewood. Hunh?"

The two rolled off side by side, Little John patting his diminutive assistant on the back in praise of his achievement—giant pats that almost sent him headlong.

"It's tradition," laughed Walter to Clement and Donald, "that Little John was once a champion feller. He could have beaten Spareribs with one hand. But those two put on a good show. Little John, big as he is, is worth his weight in silver in any camp. Every man here will work better for seeing him in action." He glanced about. "All right, men! Let's go! Space off. Watch your step. Don't forget to call as a timber starts to fall. We're off!"

With a will the men scattered to their work. The "chunk-a-chunk" of axes, the "z-zing" of saws, and the warning shouts rang through the woods. Seemingly in no time, a man was swinging a team of horses around to the end of a log, driving in the dogs attached to his hauling chain, and snaking away the timber in the direction of a rollway. Work had really begun.

All day the cheerful notes of lumbering rang through the woods. No trouble developed at any point. If Johannes was meditating mischief, he gave no sign, save for a sullen turning of his back whenever Walter came near. The crew was off to a perfect start.

Johannes and the red-haired Terry kept much together. And with them, in leisure hours and at meals, were Jules Baladieu, a big blond chap with the scarred and broken features of an experienced and tough woodsman. There was also in that little group, a thin, foxy Sam Walcott and a tall, black-haired bearded giant who bore the odd name of Toumel Rostinov. He was a quiet chap with hard dark eyes. All these men Walter studied at every opportunity. Within that group were the human explosives that might cause trouble.

One day succeeded another without trouble of any sort. The crew shook down. Production speeded up. And each night the wolf pack howled. Once or twice wolf tracks were found in the morning, near enough to camp to show that the animals were getting bolder and that they were reconnoitering the camp. Walter, fearful of an attack on his stables, armed a couple of the stablemen and saw that the horses were well shut up at night.

On the third night of lumbering, Raoul roused Walter when the light of the young moon was fading and the dark period just before the first trace of dawn was at hand. The wolf pack was particularly noisy, though it was hard to judge just where it was.

"Me, I am afraid it is the moose they drive," said Raoul anxiously.

"I've half a mind to go out," exclaimed Walter.

"It may be, by the time we get there, the damage would be done," returned Raoul. "And in the dimness we might have trouble helping. Too, the wolves might turn on us. But if we four go, armed, and with torches, it might work."

"We will try," said Walter. "I wish to save that Spirit Moose."

Quickly they roused Clement and Donald, caught up rifles and electric torches, and started out. Once in the open air, the snarls and yelps came clearer and very definitely from the direction of the moose yard. Walter set a stiff pace, and the more inexperienced members of the group were hard put to it to keep up. But they made no complaint.

They had covered barely half the distance when it suddenly became noticeable that the sounds from the wolf pack were coming from two directions.

"They've split the group," panted Raoul, "and one or two of the moose are in flight. That's rather unusual. Perhaps that wolf pack is really two that joined hunting."

The sounds of the one group grew steadily fainter, but the howls and yelps and snarls ahead grew steadily sharper. The boys tore along, heading for the little cliff over the yard. As they approached it they caught the angry bellows of the big moose. Clearly the battle was sharply joined.

The four boys rolled and tumbled down the long slope and staggered out to the edge of the cliff. Their light rays shot out over the yard below. Not strong for that distance, the beams yet disclosed the leaping, rushing, active gray shapes, darting in and out, striving to reach the three great moose who had backed in against an outjutting section of the cliff. One of these they recognized as the Spirit Moose. Even as their rays focused on the scene, they saw the great moose rear and lunge at a charging figure and send it scurrying away, yelping with pain. Then two more charged in, and the old moose met them with a sweep of his great antlers, tossing them back, one so disabled that it was instantly set upon by its mates.

Crack! The other boys, intent on watching the scene, started as Walter's rifle blazed and a wolf leader, caught in full charge, toppled heels overhead. Instantly the pack were upon him. Then Raoul fired. And suddenly the wolves realized that something was amiss. The fever of attack faded. Like drifting gray shadows, the wolves sped into the bushes and departed silently, pursued by a fusillade of shots.

"That ends that, I'm sure," said Walter. "They would have had that great old chap in the end, I fear. Wonder if he's badly hurt."

"Me, I think not," said Raoul. "Cut up, yes. That moose, he's tired, so tired he can hardly stand. I have it, Walt. Me, I'll return to camp for food for him. And I will come back and go very close while he's too tired to run away or charge. After that, he will be friendly. Me, I think so. See, he minds not even our lights."

"Take Donald with you," said Walter. "Clem and I will stay here."

Raoul nodded and started away, while Walter and his friend crouched down to watch. Already the dim light, filtering in, made the scene clearer. In every direction the snow was torn up and bloodstained. A long and terrible battle had been waged, it appeared, with loss to both sides.

Directly below, the two moose stood with legs far apart, trying to hold their weary bodies upright. Their heads hung low, though the great leader more than once tried to lift his heavy antlers and get a view upward. He was still resting, however, when Raoul and Donald reappeared. Raoul went straight towards the great beast. It waved its head in an attempt at a threat, and a *wuffle* of anger welled from its throat. But it was too weary.

Raoul stopped a little way from it, allowing the moose to gaze at him and get used to him. Then he put down his grain and other morsels very close to the beast's nose. After that he quietly withdrew.

"No danger," he said, coming around onto the cliff. "The wolves, they are gone. And the Spirit Moose, he is simply tired and surface-cut. In a few hours he will be well. We can go."

Excitedly discussing the battle, the four returned to their camp, but they slept little that night. At breakfast, Walter explained to the men what had occurred and also told of the steps Raoul was taking to tame the famous moose and turn him into a camp mascot. At that a roar of approval ran around the table.

It was just as the men were leaving that Walter caught Little John staring at him rather fixedly. The cook always promenaded around the table as the meal advanced, joking with the men, basking in their approval of his cooking, and watching to see that all needs were supplied. Now, by the faintest flicker of an eye in the direction of the cook shack, he told Walter he wished to speak with him in private. Then he continued on his jolly travels along the board.

Walter sauntered casually into the cook shack a little later and then moved on to join Little John, who was in the storeroom.

"By *gar!*" said the latter softly. "The fat, it begin to sizzle. Me, I think I poison the stew of that gang."

"Meaning Johannes and his crowd?"

"*Oui, Monsieur le Boss!* The others they joke wiz me as I go about. But Johannes—*non*—no! He drop hees voice when I come near. But ze leetle words, I catch them: 'Go easy. Our time's coming.' 'In three-four days,' or 'We catch heem when he's not looking.' Trouble, is it not, Walt? Hunh?"

"I reckon," answered Walter soberly. "Keep your ear to the ground."

Suddenly Little John shoved him aside, and his bulk filled the doorway, hiding Walter. "You, Spareribs. Why you not peeling those *pommes de terre?* Get busy, you midge! Or I put you across my knee. Scat!"

Spareribs scuttled across the room and began peeling potatoes at desperate speed.

"That's the way to boss 'em," chuckled Johannes harshly from the Mess Camp doorway. "C'n you spare a piece of tallow, Little John? Good." He grinned lazily and turned away.

Spareribs screwed up his face at the man's back, then grinned at Little John and returned to his other work.

"Johannes is the leader, of course," snapped Walter.

"He sneak in to listen, always. He stab in back. But lead? Me, I'm not sure," answered Little John.

CHAPTER VI
The Great Ice Storm

WALTER TRAMPED INTO THE woods that morning, to set his men at work, in far more sober mood than was customary with him. Trouble was brewing. Not the routine flare-ups so common in lumber camps where woodsmen lead hard lives and a physical scrap was in a way a form of recreation, a break in the monotonous drive. What as yet vaguely threatened was something underhand, sinister.

Things, he realized, had been going all too smoothly. The men obeyed orders with snap and vigor. Their spirit was excellent; no friction of any sort had developed. Even Johannes, though his manner was hostile, had appeared to do his work properly ever since that moose episode. But it was natural to have frictions, and there were none. When, for any reasons, things became hard and he had to drive, grudges would develop, and those who intended trouble would get busy.

During the morning, Walter considered the situation carefully. There seemed to him, in the end, nothing to do for the moment except watch. He decided to take his chums into his confidence. That would make four pairs of keen eyes on guard instead of one. And Little John was alert. He and his cookee were no mean helpers. As to the main force of woodsmen, he had some doubt. Many were friendly. But he was not sure which would leak his suspicions, if he took them into his inner group. He felt sure, however, that these friends in the gang would warn him if anything serious came to their notice.

After the noon meal Walter told his chums of Little John's warning and a little of his own fears. Both Raoul and Clement looked serious and anxious. As usual, however, the possibility of trouble stirred Donald to excitement.

"Just let 'em try things," he chuckled. "I hope they do. We've force enough, Walt, with your friends in the field gangs, to wipe 'em out. Give 'em rope enough, and we'll hang 'em with it."

"Of course I'll meet trouble if it comes," declared Walter, soberly. "I'm not seeking it, however. I'd rather make my record one of accomplishment without trouble, than to make it one of overcoming trouble."

"Anyhow," grinned Donald, not at all affected by this point of view, "here's where Donald Atkinson, the world's foremost woods detective, solves his greatest case."

"Rather, gets in to his neck, you mean," laughed Clement, "and makes the rest of us pull him out."

During the next day or so, several incidents occurred that were of deep interest to the boys and, to some degree to the camp force as well.

The first was the arrival of several wood-sleds with stores of provisions and special materials ordered by Walter. The little caravan arrived just at dusk, so the whole camp turned out to meet it. The boys, of course, managed to be in the van.

As the first sled drew up beside them, there was a sharp, high yelp of delight. Then something white and black shot like a comet from back of the seat, hit the frozen snow, and executed a somersault. Instantly the creature recovered and flew at Donald, leaping up into his arms.

"*Skipper!*" yelped Donald, in delight.

The little fox terrier and the boy indulged in a rough-and-tumble then and there, rolling over and over in the snow, while the woodsmen looked on, grinning broadly. Then the dog leaped madly at Walter. In turn, he scurried to Clement and then to Raoul to bestow his greetings.

Finally the live-wire creature spotted The Black Shadow, standing quietly on the edge of the circle. Instantly Skipper was tearing in mad circles around the great wolf dog and barking and yelping in wild excitement. The Black Shadow received these tokens of recognition and friendship with dignity, but his tail waved and his ears were pricked forward. The two had established a close comradeship in previous meetings.

"Now that this bundle of energy has arrived," chuckled Clement, "Donald will begin to perk up a bit. Perhaps his appetite will begin to come back."

"*By gar!*" Little John raised his arms aloft in pretended dismay. "Already he eat like seex men. Ze camp boss, he will have to send for more provisions and another cookee, *n'est-ce pas?*"

"Say, Walt," exclaimed Clement. He had stopped to stare at a part of the load of the forward sled. "What are these big runners for?"

Walter glanced up quickly. "Good!" he exclaimed. "Those are landing skis for *Redbird*. I'm going to fix her up and use her for emergencies and perhaps for reconnaissances."

When the fire season ended the previous fall, the little plane *Redbird* had been housed in a rough hangar on the shores of a lake that bordered the camp on one edge. Since she was fitted with pontoons, she was helpless for use when the lake had frozen over.

Early the next morning, Walter had a force of men cleaning away the drifts around the hangar and helping him with the substitution of the skis for the regular landing wheels. After that was completed to his satisfaction, he went over every part of the plane, testing each stay and connection. Finally he examined his motor and then ran it slowly for some time.

In late afternoon he had the ship shoved out on the ice. Then, climbing into the cockpit, he began taxiing back and forth over the lake surface, trying to get the hang of the sliding creature. Under the wind that drew down over the ice surface, he found there was a certain side drift. Also, it was more difficult to stop on skis than on wheels equipped with brakes. He finally rigged a rough drag brake to serve as a speed check.

Before dark, however, he was practising taking off and landing. He refused to take anyone with him on these first trials, knowing that he had much to learn. He made several spectacular slides and skids, indeed, before he mastered the difference between previous landing gears and this new arrangement. However, he found that his use of pontoons helped him to a certain extent.

The next day he took Clement up, and the two flew on a short trip over the limits of the camp woods. Clement used a field glass and found that if they were flying low he could make out men at work and even spot larger animals. He made out a couple of moose.

"If anyone is hanging around the camp, trying to contact with Johannes," he suggested on their return, "we may be able to spot him."

"A bare chance," said Walter. "Anyone hanging about or coming in would keep to cover. He would be suspicious of a plane, thinking it easier to be seen than it really is."

During these days Raoul had been working steadily to cultivate the confidence of the giant moose. Daily he carried it food and special dainties. While its companions had departed, it had hung around, gradually approaching nearer and nearer to the camp. Raoul made no attempt to approach too close, though he frequently stood in full sight. Presently the moose began to appear on the edge of the chopping area, staring at the busy men. It was clear that his taming was proceeding rapidly.

Very early one morning Donald stepped from his camp and proceeded over the icy paths towards the Wanigan Camp. It was one of the days when he opened early in order to meet demands of the men before they went into breakfast. The glazed ice made footing difficult, and he proceeded with the utmost care, especially when it came to rounding corners. Ahead of him, Skipper sprawled and skidded and scratched along.

The dog rounded the end of the mess camp, and Donald started to follow. At that instant Skipper loosed a yelp of sheer terror, and came slipping, sliding, scrambling back, attempting to put an all-too-short tail between his legs. He caromed off Donald's feet and upset his master.

"Wuffle!" snuffled something. Donald looked up to stare in consternation at an enormous ungainly creature with tremendous antlers that towered immediately over him. The Spirit Moose had arrived at camp!

For an instant Donald sat petrified. He expected the moose to charge, yet somehow he lacked the will to make a move. But the giant did nothing of the sort. It gave a surprised snort, than stuck down its long head with its pendulous lower lip to get a whiff of this strange creature at close hand.

And now Donald *dared* not move. Skipper, having plowed to a halt at a safe distance, and having gotten over his own fright sufficiently to be anxious for his master's safety, was barking wildly and threatening to dart in. Only uncertain footing was deterring him. But the uproar was attracting notice. Heads were appearing at the doors and windows of the men's camp. And up a path Raoul and Walter were hurrying.

"Lie still, Don!" Raoul called quietly. "Me, I think he's not ugly. Let him get your scent. Roll quick to one side, if I say so."

Slowly Raoul advanced, with Walter, more of a stranger to the big moose, keeping in the background. The moose was tamed, but its disposition might be ugly, nevertheless. And those great cutting hoofs could inflict terrible injuries. It all depended on the temper of the great beast.

Now Raoul was very close. The great moose lifted its enormous head and gazed full at him, but made no move either to advance or retreat. Very evidently, it recognized the young French Canadian.

"Slow, now, Donald," said Raoul in a conversational tone. "Roll to one side."

Donald did as directed and presently was on his feet, his cheeks rather pale, yet delight and amazement showing in his eyes.

"Who'd have thought it!" he gasped. "Raoul, you're *some* animal tamer!"

"Me, I'm not so sure," laughed Raoul, though evidently well pleased. "It is his stomach I won, my friend. And there, Little John, he help. Oh, cook!" he called. "A hunk of gingerbread for our friend."

Little John grinned and faded from view, presently to reappear with a large chunk of fresh, spicy bread. Evidently the wind carried the fragrance to the moose. It had tasted such dainties before. Its great head shifted; its nostrils dilated. Suddenly it strode forward, ignoring the men that broke ranks to let it pass, making straight for the cook.

"Stand your ground, Little John," laughed Walter.

"By *gar*!" cried Little John, thumping his chest with his free hand. "Me, I c'n cook. Hunh? Even ze wild beasts know it."

Nevertheless, he retreated a little fearfully, as the giant moose strode towards him, until he had sidled his fat figure through the doorway of the kitchen shack. From that vantage point he held out the dainty at arm's length. The moose came on, its nose outstretched. It gave an eager "wuffle." Its great jaws opened, the pendulous lip dropped, and teeth closed on the hunk of sweets.

Grinning, Little John retreated farther within. And presently the whole camp broke into a roar of laughter when the moose, considering one piece insufficient, evidently decided to seek the source of supply. It started to follow through the doorway and brought up with a thump as its enormous antlers caught against the jambs.

"Me, I think, cook," laughed Raoul, "you have one leetle pet to follow you round."

"By *gar*!" chuckled Little John. "Me, I will feed heem Spareribs an' get me a real cookee." And cook and cookee broke into hot interchanges.

The moose, finally convinced that for the moment nothing further was coming its way, turned aside and began wandering about the camp, while the men trooped noisily into breakfast. They were a jolly lot that morning. Jokes flew fast and furious, interlarded with frequent boastings that at last Camp Eighteen had a mascot worthy of it—the greatest mascot any lumber camp ever had had.

The weather moderated that morning, and low clouds settled lower. By mid-morning a heavy wet snow was falling. This stopped at sunset, and the air cooled enough to form a thick crust. But the cloud persisted all night, and by next morning a thick mist rain was falling that froze as it fell. All day it continued, gradually turning the woods into a fairyland of crystal. It grew colder that night, but the clouds broke away. When morning again came, the woods shone in dazzling splendor.

"Do you mind, Walter," asked Clement, "if Donald and I go out right after the noon meal and get a few photographs? We may not have another chance like this all winter. We'll make up time, of course."

"Okeh!" agreed Walter. "Only be watchful and don't go too far. The footing's dangerous, and I don't want either of you laid up with injuries. Moreover, the trees themselves are a source of danger, they're so heavily weighted with ice. Leave the dogs here."

"And what about a rifle for the wolves?"

"Haven't heard them ranging about for a night or so. Besides, footing is so bad they'll not be over-active." He grinned. "You're going out for trees, so you'll be near 'em. If cornered, climb up and wait until we seek you. A rifle's a dangerous thing where you're likely to fall every other step, and you may forget about safety catches. A bullet might find a mark that was not intended."

The two boys started promptly after the meal, tramping first along the lake edge and the stream. Their heavily hobnailed shoes gave them fairly secure footing, and the heavy crust bore them up. So the going was comparatively easy. The subjects for photography were so many and beautiful that gradually they were tolled farther and farther from camp. They finally awoke with a start to the fact that they were more than two miles from home.

"We'd better be making tracks for camp," said Clement. "We can go around by the edge of the swampland."

"Let's cut straight through the woods by way of Stony Brook trail," amended Donald. "I'm tired, and I want to get back."

"Right-o!" agreed Clement, thrashing his arms. "*Phew!* It's sure growing colder; and the sky looks like snow flurries."

"Brrrrr!" shivered Donald. "There's a breath of icy wind now. Hustle! A red-hot camp stove sounds good to me."

They speeded up, conscious of a strong breath of air drawing in. The ice-laden branches of the trees about them scraped and snapped. From somewhere near came the sharp crackling report of falling dead timber.

Again the wind ceased while the boys made time. Then came a real gust. Instantly, all about them sounded several dozen crackling reports. Just ahead, a great bough broke loose, with a sharp bark like a field piece, and thudded to the ground, spraying bits of ice like shrapnel all around.

Don glanced up in sudden uneasiness. "Not so good, Clem!" he exclaimed. "Hope that wind holds back until we get out of this."

"Don't go so fast, you won't have time to dodge, if necessary," Clem called after his speeding chum. "If the wind really comes, things will be popping all around us. Listen!" he cried. "There comes a real gust."

They heard the eery sound of the wind as it came swooping in and played on the frozen strings the tree-tops provided. But almost at once the musical note was smothered by reports like musketry—snappings, cracklings, jarring thuds. That ice-laden forest, dangerously overloaded, was yielding before the added strain the wind imposed.

The uproar deepened, rolled nearer. The two boys instinctively drew closer together. They stared upward, fascinated, watching the branches bend and writhe, or snap sharply, startlingly, and plunge downward. Showering ice particles stung their upturned cheeks.

Cra-ack! A great bough immediately above them snapped off short and came thudding down, striking and carrying away a lesser branch as it fell. The boys made desperate leaps in different directions. Yet one fork sent Clement sprawling headlong and a switching branchlet raised a stinging welt on Donald's cheek.

"Shelter!" gasped the other, staggering to his feet. "We've got to find shelter."

"There isn't any near here—no cliffs or anything," cried Clement. "Just go as fast as we can until the next blast comes; then stop and be ready to dodge."

They sped on, slipping, sliding, anxious. Weakened branches were falling at intervals, now, even between gusts. Faint through the woods came another sound—the reverberating clangor of the great triangle at camp, singing under lusty blows.

"They're—calling in—the men," panted Donald, as they paused, hugging a great tree trunk, for another gust to pass.

A sharp report sounded directly overhead. They leaped aside, barely in time to avoid a bough that slid straight down the trunk. Ice was crackling and falling everywhere. Wherever they looked branches were being carried away.

"Must be something like fighting through a barrage," exclaimed Donald. He was white with excitement, not unmixed with fear; but the thrill of it all gripped him.

"Hurry—*hurry!*" cried Clement. "And we'll stay some distance apart, Don. It wouldn't do for a bough to catch us both."

On, on they sped, twenty feet apart, checking only when the heavy gusts roared in, and dodging, rather than progress, became the order of the moment.

Presently, above Donald's head, a tremendous bough let go with a terrific and startling report.

"To your left, Don!" shrieked Clement. He checked the impulse to spring forward. Donald leaped, but an instant's hesitation lost him his chance. He fell, but had only begun to pick himself up when the enormous branch sent him crashing and dropped across his body. He lay motionless.

With his heart in his throat, Clement leaped forward, unmindful of the hail of ice fragments showering down, and of lesser branches falling all about. Desperately he pulled and broke branches; then he chopped madly with the little camp ax he carried in his belt. Fortunately the main stem had not fallen across his chum. It was a lesser bough that had felled him. Quickly, after all, Clem freed him and dragged him to one side.

Then Donald stirred. "Why—what—what——" he murmured dazedly.

"Steady, Don!" said Clement shakily. "Bough took you down. Get your breath, then see if you can move all your limbs."

Donald complied, but still a little uncertainly. Presently, with the other's help, he clambered to his feet and stood leaning against a tree.

"Just a brief—knockout," he said at last. "Feel sort of sore but the old joints appear to work. It's lucky we separated, Clem. Come on. I can travel. It's less than a mile to camp now."

The increasing wind was working more havoc with each passing moment, but somehow the boys managed to escape further threats, and at last they came out on the edge of the section where chopping was going on. Here, of course, there was much less overhead to endanger them, and they made faster progress, though Donald moved unsteadily, as if shaken by his experience.

Suddenly he stopped and pointed with a shaking finger to the edge of the uncut timber. "*Look!*" he gasped.

A crumpled figure lay stretched face down on the icy surface.

CHAPTER VII
Redbird Proves Itself a Snowbird

CLEMENT SPRANG FORWARD AND was first to kneel at the side of the stricken figure. He swung it over on its back by main strength just as Donald arrived.

"Jean!" gasped the latter.

Clement nodded as his fingers made a swift examination. "He looks badly hurt, Don. Probably hit by that bough of the tree, right back there, and staggered out this far before he collapsed. Suppose you go on to camp, and I'll stay here until you send out help. Tell Walter to send a hand sled. Can you make it all right?"

"Sure!" agreed Donald instantly. "I'll go as fast as possible." He turned and started away.

"Don't take too many chances," Clement called after him. "And have someone look you over when you get in."

Donald waved a hand and stumbled and skidded on down the trail. Clement again gave attention to the still figure before him. Jean's face was very white, but he breathed faintly. Clement saw that he was well wrapped, using his own Mackinaw to help. Then he started to chafe the injured man's limbs, striving to restore and keep up circulation until help should come.

"It seems sort of strange to me," he muttered as he worked. "If that bough had hit him square, it would have felled him in his tracks. Must have been a glancing blow. And where's his ax? I wonder——" He stared thoughtfully at some scratches on the snow surface, barely visible under the powdery coating of a light snow flurry.

In his anxiety for Jean, and for Donald as well, hours seemed to pass before, far towards camp, he heard faint halloos. He answered eagerly. Presently three figures broke from the woods. One drew a hand sled. As they came nearer, Clement made out Walter pressing forward in the lead, followed by Black Mike and Jerry. Walter spotted his chum at once and waved his hand. He speeded up again, quickly outdistancing his companions.

"Serious?" he demanded, as he came up.

"I'm afraid so," declared Clement. "I can't rouse him. How's Donald?"

"Nothing more serious than a shake-up," said Walter, as he knelt beside Jean. "He'll be all right after a little rest. But Jean's badly off, I can see. We'll hustle him to camp."

"Send him back by the others and stay back here a minute," said Clement.

Walter gave him a keen glance and nodded.

In a moment or so the others arrived, and Jean was tenderly lifted onto the sled and wrapped in heavy blankets that Walter had remembered to bring. After that he was strapped securely in place, to avoid further injury if the sled should skid, and was started back to camp. Walter remained looking off quietly until the men with the sled had disappeared around a bend.

"What's up, Clem?" he demanded then.

"How do you think Jean met his injury?" asked Clement.

"At first glance," said Walter, "it looks as if he had been struck by that tree bough, over there, and had staggered a little distance before falling."

"If so," retorted Clement, "why isn't there a scratch in the snow—some mark of his hobnails? He would have shuffled, if injured."

Walter verified that. Also he began to glance about, shooting keen glances here and there. "The next natural supposition is that he slipped and fell on the ice."

"But when I found him," answered Clement, "he was lying face down, although the injury appears to be at the back of his head. He might have thrashed over, of course."

"Not likely," said Walter thoughtfully, "not if stunned by a fall. He would have flattened out. I notice his ax isn't here. Probably, when he heard the triangle signal, he dropped it and tramped out this way to be sure all men had gone back. But that's odd. A woodsman is inclined to keep his ax until he gets to camp. What else have you up your sleeve, Clem?"

"This," said Clement. And now there was ill-concealed excitement in his tones. "There's been a faint snow flurry in the last half hour. Whatever happened to Jean happened before that; and if the flurry hit here when it blew over us in the woods, it fell before you called in the men. There was snow powder over Jean."

"You're using your head, Clem," complimented Walter. "He came over here, then, before work stopped. He was chopping some hundred yards from here. One question is, what brought him?"

"I've gone a little farther," went on Clement. "If you look carefully, under the snow powder from where Jean's feet lay back towards the left, I think you will see scratches. I haven't traced them, but I have a hunch as to what happened."

Instantly Walter was on the scent. Dropping to his knees and putting his head close to the icy surface, he blew off the powder, step by step, and studied scratches now clearly visible. These he traced back to the edge of the woods, where grew an enormous oak. After a moment he looked up, his eyes hot. "Come here, Clem," he called.

Clement came running over.

"I think I see what you saw," Walter went on then. "You think Jean fell or was knocked down some distance from where he was found and dragged over to make it appear he had been struck a glancing blow by that bough? I agree. He was dragged from this oak; and behind this oak are other hobnail marks. Someone lay in wait and struck him as he passed."

Clement nodded.

"That raises questions. Personal enmity or general camp trouble? We'll have to nose out what enemies Jean had in camp. Not many, I'm sure. He's popular. Was Jean trailing someone? And did that one spot him and take cover? And was that individual a member of our camp, or was he, say, the ski-runner? And if he wished it to appear that Jean was struck by the bough, why did he leave him some steps away from it?"

"One answer is that the assailant heard or saw someone else approaching or passing near and thought it wise to depart hurriedly."

"Good," said Walter. "Tell you what. I've got to get back to camp, and you've had enough. I'll ask you to remain a few minutes while I return and send Raoul out to do what trailing he can. He can beat any of us, except Indian Pete, and he's not available. Then you come back to camp. I'm anxious about Jean. By hurrying, I can reach camp by the time the men get in with him. Okeh?"

"Sure!" agreed Clement.

"Watch your step," said Walter a little anxiously. "The trouble-maker may still be about, watching to see what takes place. Don't let anyone sneak up on you."

"I'll be on guard," Clement assured him.

Walter nodded and hurried away, his long legs carrying him far more swiftly than the men with the sled could travel over the dangerous surface. So he found himself coming in on their heels and able to help in settling Jean comfortably on a couch in the little camp hut that was reserved for cases of sickness or injury.

Swiftly Walter made his examination and applied such means of first aid as seemed appropriate. But Jean remained completely out. Then Walter sent for Little John. The elephantine cook was as capable as he was large in many ways, and not the least in his ability to aid in cases of accident.

Little John's examination was thorough and long continued, and steadily he became more serious. Finally he looked up. "Me, I think heem bad hurt," he announced. "His skull, she may be fractured; or Jean, he may be stunned, con—con——"

"Concussion," supplied Walter. "He needs a doctor's care, doesn't he, Little John?"

Little John nodded. "But the wire, she is down," he reminded.

"I know," said Walter. "Worse yet, the camp doctor at Camp Fifteen met with an injury, I was told by the last men in. There's no one near at hand. What about moving him out, Little John?"

"Jean, he should not be move'," asserted the cook, "unless le docteur, he can't get here."

"I'll start down trail with a message," exclaimed Don, who was standing by.

"You're hardly in shape, Don," said Walter. "We've got to get a doctor here, if possible, and without delay. It's up to me. I'll fly out for one and bring him back. And I must leave at once."

Donald gave a gasp of protest, and Little John looked up and shook his head. "Non, no!" he said. "One life, perhaps, is enough, Walt. The gale, she come fast. To fly, it will be dangerous, n'est-ce pas? Your life, Walt, she is worth too much."

"I can make it," said Walter quietly. "When the need is great we forget the risk. Little John, I'm counting on you. If I'm delayed for any reason and am not back by dark, and Jean has not come to, start him down the trail with the best men we have. Tell them to travel all night and pass him along to other sled crews at Camp Sixteen. Keep him moving." He turned. "Donald, tell Black Mike to get Raoul and Clement back at once. I want to see them, and Black Mike when he gets back. I'll be down at the hangar."

Swiftly Walter prepared for his journey. There was no doubt in his mind but that he was going into danger. At the same time, he knew he must go. He was responsible for his men. Need had arisen. He must meet it. It was not going to be an easy flight. The gusts were increasing with every moment. Snow flurries were threatening, and by night a full gale would be roaring in. His plane was very light and not very heavily powered. Every minute would count.

"Keep watch here in camp, Little John," he said, as, muffled in his winter flying suit and with a bundle of wraps for the passenger he hoped to bring back, he stopped for one more look at the unconscious Jean.

"Me, I watch heem," declared Little John, bestowing a bone-crushing hand-grip on his young boss. "And, Walt, you make ze plane behave." His anxiety showed in every line of his face. Gone was all jollity in a shell of anxiety and dread.

Walter forced a cheery smile and hurried down to the hangar, picking up one or two helpers on the way. He had his motor well warmed when Raoul and Clement and Black Mike came running up. He took them aside and swiftly explained the circumstances.

Raoul's expression, and Clement's too, was anxious. But neither attempted any protest. They knew Walter too well; and either, in his heart, knew that he would have acted the same way under the circumstances.

"Time to hear what I find?" asked Raoul.

"No," said Walter. "Seconds count, with this rising wind. Keep it for my return. Little John has my orders about Jean, if I am not able to get back by dark. Raoul, you are in my place while I am gone. In case of necessity, Black Mike, I want you to act as field boss to direct the regular work."

Black Mike stared in utter surprise. Responsibility had never been placed on his shoulders before. He stiffened a bit. His eyes thanked Walter, but no words came.

Walter knew better than to prolong any parting. Life and death hung in the balance for Jean; and for the flyer, as well. All sensed it. They might not all meet again. Their hands clasped; they exchanged long, deep glances, and then Walter climbed over into his seat and adjusted his belt. He waved his hand to his friends and then to the gang of woodsmen who had gathered to see him off. His motor roared to a deeper note. The plane glided, with runners screeching, out onto the frozen lake surface.

Once out into the open, Walter cast an appraising eye at the blue sky above, studded with black ominous snow clouds to the west. He waited for a heavy wind gust to pass, steadying his plane as best he could as it was pulled about. Then he taxied well down the lake and swung about to face into the wind for the take-off.

Again a pounding gust roared in. He fought it as it twitched and twirled at the plane, half lifting it from the ice and almost tossing it over on one wing. But as the gust passed, he managed to straighten out and speed swiftly down the lake. The plane rose sharply, and he circled up and over the dark specks that were his friends. Then he headed for the distant bulwark of the Carter Mountains.

At first he experienced, as always, the thrill of a trip through the air. Then, all in an instant, he was flying blindly in a swirling mass of snow that seemed to choke and smother him. For two minutes this continued; then he shot clear of the cloud and found the great, far-extending range of the Carter Mountains perceptibly nearer.

Walter felt his nerves grow tense and his fingers tighten on the controls as he headed his little biplane for Wind Gap, the only real break in this towering range. At first he had intended shooting high over the mountains, but on gaining altitude he had found the air currents far more dangerous than lower down. His problem, now, was to get through the gap between squalls. Flying over or through the gap would be difficult enough at best. The break well deserved its name.

Steadily the depths of the gap opened up before him. But the black clouds of another squall were closing in on him. A swift glance backward showed him much of the landscape cut off by a white curtain. This squall was wider and more extensive than any previous one of the afternoon. His lips compressed into a thin line. He nursed his motor, striving to gain the last ounce of speed, while the white curtain raced with him for the gap entrance.

Seemingly by yards only, he made it, and saw on either side the towering cliffs that bounded the gap. At once his ship began to pitch and toss violently. At times it swerved towards the cliffs as if drawn by a magnet. An instant later it might be tossed violently away. Walter had to draw on the last atom of his skill to meet each new buffet and wrench as the boiling, churning winds tossed the plane about like a chip in a rushing stream. Farther along the course, the ship dropped down air pockets with the speed of an express elevator. Again, it rocketed dizzily upward. At other times it was projected forward as if propelled from a cannon. But it was a staunch little craft and Walter was its master. With arms aching from the strain and nerves ragged, Walter shot the red creature out the far end of the gap and over the flatter open country beyond. In the far distance he made out a low-lying smudge of smoke. That must be the mill town of Wilkinsville, for which he was headed.

Sput—sput-er—sput—sput!

A shiver of fear punctured Walter's feeling of relief. The even note of his motor had broken without warning. Desperately he manipulated his gas, the while his anxious eyes scanned his instrument board. For a moment the motor's note improved; then again it faltered. It appeared to be trouble with his gas—a clogged feed pipe or—— Vibration became noticeable. The motor coughed and labored.

"I've got to go down," he told himself.

He stared ahead and downward, striving to plan his action. He could never make the miles to the next lake or to a good landing field. He fought the temptation to bail out; that would mean the certain destruction of his plane. Too, it might mean the death of Jean. Until the last instant, he told himself, he must fight on. Again his anxious gaze swept the wood and brushlands below.

Then he spotted it—the one real break, a far-outlying farm. He must try to land on its fields.

Desperately Walter continued his struggle with the controls, striving to keep the ship on even keel as its speed fell off. Twice he pulled the boat out of an incipient spin. For an instant the edge of a snow flurry enveloped him and the fear shook him that he would crash in that snow curtain. But it drifted off, and he found himself nearer those open fields.

His coughing, laboring motor stalled. The sudden silence was broken only by the whistle of the wind through the stays. Again he barely avoided a nose dive as the ground rushed up to meet him.

"I'm going to crash!" The thought flashed through his mind. "I can't avoid it."

Yet he kept on striving, white-lipped, calling upon his last shreds of nerve and skill. Somehow he succeeded in partially leveling off. It was as if his very will lifted that dipping nose. Still, the ship struck hard. It leaped high as it hit some obstruction or ridge. Again it struck, tilted dangerously, righted at last, slithered sideways as some faint rut caught a runner. But, though winded from the shock of landing hard, and half draped over the cockpit, Walter still did the right things and kept the craft on its keel.

His speed was decreasing when, with another wind blast, thick snow clouds enveloped him. Through the driving flakes he made out vague forms taking shape ahead. The plane was still sliding fast enough under the impetus of the wind to suffer damage in a collision. Walter worked to check and turn his craft. He made out those obstructions, now. One was a barn; the other was a giant straw stack. With one last desperate effort he swerved the plane from the path of the barn and headed it into the stack. *Redbird* hit, nose on. It rebounded, teetered for an instant like a sandpiper, and came to a standstill.

CHAPTER VIII
Boom!

BADLY SHAKEN, BUT WITH unspeakable relief, Walter climbed out over the cockpit and sagged weakly to the ground. For a minute he lay there, getting his breath and recovering his self-control. He was still slumped against a runner when a young man came sprinting around the barn.

"Hurt?" he inquired anxiously.

Walter shook his head. "I'll be all right—in a minute."

"Dang it!" exclaimed the stranger, a sandy-haired chap with reddish eyes, now lit with excitement. "You were lucky to make it! Don't see how you did, in this wind. Spotted you up there and knew you were in trouble. Then I lost you in the snow flurry and thought you must have crashed for sure. Guess it wasn't all luck. Must have taken nerve and skill. What happened, anyhow?"

"Trouble with the feed pipe; either clogged or broken," explained Walter, dragging himself to his feet and wavering uncertainly once he found himself on them. "I must mend it and take off at once."

"In this weather, and with you in that shape?" exclaimed the stranger. "Nothing doing! You put up with me. I'm all alone today and itching for company."

"Many thanks," exclaimed Walter heartily. "Under ordinary circumstances, I'd accept in an instant. But I'm on a matter of life and death."

"May be a matter of death for you if you try," snapped the young man.

"Still, I must try," said Walter. "You can help me, if you will."

"Anything you say," responded the other, still with protest in his tones.

Walter found himself steadying, despite the nerve shock due to experiencing, under such dangerous circumstances, his first forced landing. Now he found a surge of thankfulness rushing through his being. He had a feeling he was going to make it yet.

A quick examination disclosed a broken feed pipe, probably damaged in one of the wrenching twists the plane had undergone. Fortunately, Walter carried spare pipe of this nature. So he set to work without delay to remove the defective section and replace it with a new one. In this operation, he found his companion no mean helper. He had not tinkered over farm motors for nothing.

The feed pipe repaired and tested, Walter went over the entire machine with the utmost care. He found stay wires that needed attention, and one runner required straightening. Then his companion led him out into the fields and showed him the best and smoothest area for a take-off.

"I can make it here," Walter said, at last, "provided you have a team to haul my plane out into position. I'll gladly settle with you."

"Not a red cent," laughed the other. "Gee! I'm getting a great kick out of all this. It fractures the monotony all right. I still wish you could stay. Can't you change your mind?"

"On occasion, yes," laughed Walter. "But not this time. I must get back to the Northrop Camps with a doctor. And the sooner I make it, with this rising gale, the better."

"The Northrop Camps!" exclaimed the young fellow. "Then you came through or over Wind Gap in this gale. I'll say you have your nerve with you. Sounds like some doings of Big Jim Northrop or his son Walter. I expect you know 'em."

"I happen to be Big Jim's son," laughed Walter, with that thrill of happiness that always flowed over him when others mentioned his father.

"I'll be jiggered!" exclaimed the other. "To think that Walter Northrop should actually land on our place! It's a red-letter day for Guy Parker, all right!"

"I'll be glad to have Guy Parker drop into our camp—Camp Eighteen—any time this winter," laughed Walter, "and give me a chance to return some of the courtesies he is showing me."

"I may, at that," grinned Guy. "Only it won't be in just the fashion you set coming down here. Now, let me hitch up a team to haul your plane out to the field."

He hustled off around the barn and presently returned driving a two-horse team. The horses were somewhat skittish, not a little fearful of the wide-winged creature to which they were backed. But finally they settled down, and the drag out to the field began. Here, again, there were delays, as several panels of two fences had to be removed to let the plane through. But finally *Redbird* was in position for flight, at one end of an all-too-short field.

That short take-off worried Walter considerably. With so little help at hand, there was no way to chock the runners and release them quickly. Finally he thought to tie a rope to the frame of his plane and run it back to a stout tree. Near the plane, he ran the rope over a stump and stationed Guy there with an ax.

"When my motor is running right and the wind is right, too, I'll signal with a wave of the hand. At that signal, chop the rope through. That will release me quickly, which is what I want. Now—" he held out his hand—"hearty thanks for all your help. About that look-in at camp, I mean it. Just go to the nearest point on our logging road and tell any camp boss that Walt says to pass you up. Good-bye!"

He climbed up into the cockpit and revved his motor. A wind gust whistled by. The wind steadied. He raised his hand and waved it. Out of the back of his eye he saw the ax crashing downward. It cut cleanly, for the ends of the rope whipped back with sharp reports, and *Redbird* surged forward. Off again!

Swaying, sidling, leaping over the rough field, the little plane slid down the slight slope, gaining speed with every yard. Just as she appeared to be about to crash into the bushes and small trees that lined the far fence, Walter pulled back on the stick, and *Redbird* rose gracefully, her runners just tickling the tips of the highest branches. Swiftly she gained altitude. Then Walter swung around, swooped by the farm, again waved a "good-bye," and was away as fast as he could travel towards the smoke smudge that marked Wilkinsville.

Steadily the smoke patch grew larger. Within fifteen minutes, Walter was circling about outside of town, looking over the frozen surface of a lake near its borders and selecting a landing point. He made his landing easily, this time, and taxied swiftly up to the nearest shore building that showed signs of life. Here he quickly got men to watch his plane and another man to drive him to a young doctor whom he knew.

He was fortunate in finding Doctor Maclaren at home, and ready, as soon as circumstances were explained to him, to take the risky trip out to camp.

"I've only had one or two experiences in a plane," he laughed, "so I'm not sure how good a sailor I'll prove to be."

"You'll know after you get in," laughed Walter. "Don't be disturbed if we do all sorts of circus tricks. We'll get through." He thought it inadvisable to explain just what had happened on the way in. "If you're ready, we'll get going. My camp men are under orders to start the injured man down to civilization if I'm not back by dark."

They hurried back to the lake, and Walter swiftly bundled his passenger into the rear seat, after seeing to it that he was well protected against the cold. The take-off was made without trouble, but once aloft, Walter realized that the gale was growing in force with each passing moment, and that the snow clouds were heavier and more threatening. He gained altitude and sped towards the Gap with all the power he could get from *Redbird's* motor.

"I'll have to get up high, wind or no wind," he told himself, "and go well over the range."

Swiftly the Carter Mountains rose higher and higher before him, with only that one notch in their long barricade. But he was miles away when a flurry closed in on him, dense, blinding, and more wet than usual. The plane pitched badly and was less responsive as the snow clung to the wings. Moreover, his instrument board was acting up.

He was tempted to turn back, but need seemed to drive him on. He was flying blind, but he had taken his compass direction from the Gap before the snow closed in. Now, in the howling wind blasts, he knew he must be driven off course. And he realized, with a shock of fear, that his altimeter was not registering properly. With wings weighted by snow, was he high enough to avoid crashing on the mountain sides? Desperately he tried to claw higher. Utterly blind as he was, and with the plane so tossed about, it seemed to him equally risky to turn back or go forward. Which was "back," anyhow?

All at once his ship appeared to drop from under him. Then it leaped dizzily upward. Again it wrenched and twisted. It bucked like a wall-eyed broncho. Twice, but for his safety strap, he would have been tossed out. He was in Wind Gap again, but this time flying blind!

Determinedly he struggled to control the wild thing he rode. Not alone for his own sake, but for Jean's and the doctor's must he win through. He forced from his mind the sense of the nearness of those threatening cliffs. He sought to rise, ever rise, in the teeth of that roaring whistling gale. The thirty seconds of that storm-driven passage seemed an hour, before a lessening of violent motion told him he had won through.

But now, as he set his course for camp, a new fear beset him. With each passing minute he was a mile and a half nearer Camp Eighteen. But in this veil of driving snow, how was he to recognize it, how effect a landing? And beyond, if he overran, was only wilderness. The miles were melting away. Nearer—nearer——

Unexpectedly the flurry lightened. For the briefest instant he looked down on a huddle of lumber camps, a bit of stream. Then they were as instantly veiled from sight. But he had recognized them. Camp Fourteen! That helped to orient him.

The gale blew ever harder. The snow was powdery now, and dryer. With the help of the wind it was scouring off the wetter snow. He was fighting into the teeth of the gale. He wondered what speed he was making. He tried to compute on the basis of Wind Gap to Camp Fourteen. At most, he was not many minutes from home.

The snow ever thickened and lightened. The wind rose steadily, less gusty. Clear sky and bitter cold were coming. Again he caught a fleeting glimpse downward. Forest, endless forest!

Once more the curtain smothered. Again it lifted. A spotted stream course. It was gone before he could recognize it. Another bunch of log structures, a wooded stretch, a cut-over section. Probably Camp Sixteen, but he could not be sure. Yet again the vague view opened—to clutching branches of a giant veteran of the forest, not a hundred feet below. In a panic he struggled upward. His motor labored under the strain.

Again the view formed indistinctly as he peered over the cowl. Some lake, it appeared. He debated landing to see where he was. All at once he shook his head to clear it. Was he seeing things? A dancing black speck whirled and circled over the icy expanse. And suddenly thankfulness and utter relief welled up in his heart. That whirling figure had been instantly lost to sight, but not before he had recognized it. Just so The Black Shadow had been accustomed to come out on the ice and dance and bark as he came in from a flight. That was Beaver Lake. He was home.

He banked and began a slow circling, waiting for the flurries to lift and give him a clear view for landing. He knew the sound of his plane would have been heard in camp and that no start would be made to remove Jean, even if he had to stay aloft until after dusk, now not far distant.

As a matter of fact, the thought had hardly flashed through his mind when the flurry swept aside, as a drapery might be snatched back by a human hand, and the lake surface lay clear before him. Along its edge black dots were gathering. The camp force was coming down to give a welcome.

At once Walter banked his plane and swooped downward. It was not a very good landing that he made; in fact, it was so poor a one that he almost upset, running for some distance on a single runner. Then the other slammed back on the ice, and he taxied over to the gang of woodsmen, who were cheering lustily.

Clement was first at the plane, reaching up a hand, but so overcome he could not speak. His face showed the strain he had been under. Raoul, too, let his manner rather than his words show his deep feeling. But Donald blurted out, "Gee! Walt! You've had us scared stiff, as this gale increased and these flurries kept coming."

"Well, I'm back—that's the main thing." He leaned over to help the doctor release his belt and then to steady him over the side. As the latter released the flaps of his helmet, it was clear to see that he was white and shaken. Yet he forced a grin.

"If that's your sport of flying," he said, "I've had enough of it. Still, 'twas an adventure! I imagine it took real skill and nerve to come through that."

"A close shave," returned Walter soberly, "more than once. I'll be able, however, to take you back in better weather, I'm sure." He turned to Little John. "How's Jean?"

"No change!" said the cook.

"We'll look him over at once," suggested Doctor Maclaren.

Walter led the way to the little hut, and the doctor began his examination. He was thoughtful and grave when finally he looked up. "Concussion," he announced. "There appears to be no fracture. He will come out of this, but how soon I can't say. I'll be here overnight, of course, and I'll know better as to his chances in the morning. With trails in such dangerous condition, I wouldn't advise moving him, however."

Doctor Maclaren proved an interested and an interesting guest at dinner and during the evening. He was curious to see everything and quick to take his part in the conversation of any group.

"Me, I think he would make a good camp doctor," said Raoul in an aside to Walter, as the evening meal progressed.

"I agree," said Walter, watching the young medical man as he joked with the near-by woodsmen. "We may get him a place before long. I——" He stopped and gazed up and down the length of the tables. "Raoul, do you see what I do?"

Raoul's glance sped around the room. He looked down at his plate as he said quietly, "Me, I think so. The trouble gang, it is broken up."

"That's it; they've scattered among the other men."

"Good thing, isn't it?" said Donald, who had overheard. "They won't be all the time planning trouble."

"Probably their planning is completed," returned Walter soberly, "and action is beginning. A half a dozen little centers are harder to watch than one larger center. Since the Johannes crowd made the move, I'd say the purpose was to get closer to more of the other men and to foment trouble."

"Why not throw 'em out and be done with 'em?" demanded Donald.

"I must first be *sure*," said Walter, "so that no injustice may be done. To simply let them out might mean transferring trouble-makers to some other camp. Raoul, we're far enough away not to be overheard. What did you find this afternoon?"

"Me, I am not sure; the signs on the hard surface, they were not too clear. But, my friend, I see it this way. A man, he sneak from his chopping post. Jean, he see him and follow. The man, he find he is followed and he hide and surprise Jean. He strike heem down and drag heem towards that fallen bough. He intend to put heem under it. But me, I think he is scared away. He leave heem and go into thick bushes. He hide for a time, but whoever it was did not see Jean.

"Then the attacker, he creep away through cover and go on away from camp. Soon he meet up with another man. That man come on skis. They talk. Money passes."

"How do you know that?" demanded Donald excitedly.

"Quiet," cautioned Walter. "Show no special interest; we may be watched."

Under the edge of the table Raoul's hand moved from his own pocket to Walter's and thrust something in. "By that, which you will look at later. It is a five-dollar bill, a new one. Evidently it blow away when they count it."

"That might be helpful," murmured Walter, glancing casually about the room.

"Me, I think so," responded Raoul, and sent a laughing quip at some woodsmen down the table. Then he went on, "They part, and the attacker, he comes towards camp, but by roundabout ways. The other go off, straight into the wilderness, Walt. And soon, because of the falling snow, I lose those faint scratches."

"So he goes out and then circles around either to some other of our camps or down to Oddie's territory," said Walter.

"Me, I am not at all sure where he come from. There is just one thing more, Walt. As I give up ze trail, me, I think I hear something, very faint, far off. I may be mistaken, for the wind it make much noise, and the falling branches. Me, I think it sound like a plane—not a plane passing, but one taking off."

"Phe-ew!" Walter whistled softly and thoughtfully. "So someone else was aloft on this bad day! Might have come from any direction to a lake within tramping distance of the camp. When the weather improves, I'll move around a bit with *Redbird*, I'm thinking. What do——"

Boom!

The deep, reverberating note sounded near at hand. It was followed by odd rumbling, pounding, crackling, thumping sounds. In the instant while the men froze in their places, startled, it seemed that the ground shook slightly. Then the rush and thump of heavy-shod feet and excited cries drowned other notes as the woodsmen ran for the door.

Walter, cutting through the cook shack, collided with Clement in the doorway.

"Trouble has arrived," he snapped. "Eyes open, Clem!"

CHAPTER IX
Troubles Multiply

As Walter shot from the door of the cook shack and sped around front, the men began streaming from the main doorway of the mess shack. One had caught up a pitch torch—a number of which were always kept ready—and touched it off and was now sprinting down a path.

"Sounds like trouble at a rollway, men!" came the hoarse tones of Johannes.

Walter sped by the main crowd and caught up with the torch-bearer. After him came Raoul and Clement. Donald was slower, having stopped to get an electric torch.

Presently it was evident that Johannes had been right. Where the first great pile of logs had been stacked, in readiness to send down the stream at spring high water, there was now just a gap. As more torches appeared and men started a fire on the crest of the long rollway slope, the situation became clear. Down that slope all the logs had shot, skidding, leaping, as the snow marks showed. A few lay sprawled along the lower reaches of the grade, but many had piled up in the stream bed at all angles. They lay there like a handful of giant jackstraws, all in a tangle. The small remainder had hurtled on into the woods and brush on the far side.

"Oh, well," laughed Donald, "what's the difference? We would have sent them down later, anyhow. No harm done! Gee! I wish I'd been here, though, to see 'em let go."

"At spring high water, it would have made no difference, provided the men were ready for the drive," responded Raoul. "But now it make much trouble. Me, I think Walt will say every log must be snaked out of that river bed. Me, I tell you; it is this way. As ice melts and the water, it slowly rises, it will bring drift. That drift, it will pile up against that mass. Soon there will be a real jam, and the river, it will be choked. And what logs break free will go a little way and ground at next low water. They too will make trouble."

"I see." Donald sobered. "Seems if I'm always thinking only halfway through."

Walter came over, sniffing the air. "Powder, or a low charge of dynamite, I'd say, Raoul. Powder, I think, for this—" he showed a fragment of ropy substance—"looks like ordinary fuse. Base and key logs blown out!"

"What about the other stacks?" exclaimed Donald excitedly. "Are they likely to go sky-hooting down any minute?"

"If charges had been laid and fuses lit, they would have gone by this time," said Walter. "I'll have 'em watched tonight and examined by daylight. Raoul, keep an eye on them until I make arrangements. We——"

"Careless stacking, Boss!" interrupted Johannes in a sneering tone as he came by. Terry, who was with him, grinned but appeared uneasy.

"Me, I think Terry have something that troubles his mind," commented Raoul.

"We'll have some sort of a check-up when we get back in our own hut," said Walter. "I'm trying to picture just who was in that mess camp when the charge went off."

From men of known loyalty, Walter selected guards to watch over the remaining stacks. However, he expected no further trouble that night. Then he called the other men off and sent them back to the Men's Camp. After that he took the doctor back to the emergency camp, where he would spend the night in touch with Jean. Finally he returned to the boys' camp and found his friends eagerly awaiting him.

"Trouble has begun," he remarked, as he dropped wearily onto a bench. "The maker of it goes out on his ear the moment I'm sure of him. But I must make no mistakes. There are very few at whom I can safely point a finger of suspicion. Johannes is, of course, a natural-born trouble-maker. Terry Connors is a devil-may-care chap who would mix in for the sport of it. Ole Newson, of our old men, has a bad record. So far he has only been sullen. Then there are Jules Baladieu and Toumel Rostinov, who gang with Johannes. The others of the new men parted company promptly with that group."

"Rostinov is that big black-bearded fellow," reminded Raoul, "who held Johannes back that first night."

"That might let him out," suggested Donald.

"He might have thought the time for trouble had not arrived," Clement suggested.

Walter nodded. Clement's mind showed ever increasing power to grasp possibilities. "These men," Walter directed, "we shall watch without appearing to watch. We shall keep an eye on all others except those of known friendliness and loyalty. You have the payroll in your record books, Clement. Get it. We'll check over the names, one by one."

This was soon done. Then Walter took out the five-dollar bill which Raoul had found. "Brand new and uncreased," he commented. "We will need to know who has fresh banknotes. The serial number of this bill is B11256477. Since the notes are new, others may be around this number, for they would probably be paid out consecutively. They are issued by the First National of Warrenton. That helps, too. Of course, we can't be sure, though, that this will lead us anywhere. Its finding suggests a payment, but not necessarily all in fives of this order. I wonder how they came to lose this."

"Me, I can guess," said Raoul. "There were many calk marks. Me, I think money change hands, and as it is counted, some blows away in a gust, and this note they do not find."

"Sounds reasonable," agreed Walter. "Donald, you keep an eye on money taken in at the Wanigan Camp. The rest of us will be on the watch for money changing hands within camp. And now, let's turn in. I've had enough for one day."

That was a good deal for Walter to admit. But he really felt more done in than he dared let the others know. The attack on Jean, the strain of his trip for the doctor, the evening's episode, and Raoul's news had all laid their mark upon him. Even after the lights were out, he lay restless and wakeful in his bunk.

Outside were many sounds, in which the clangor of the gale took first place. The wind whistled and shrieked through the trees and moaned through cracks in the eaves. The gusts pounded the roofs like giant mailed fists. Ice, dislodged from the few trees left standing within the building area, rattled against roof and window. The sharp reports of snapping timber came from the near-by woods. And in the lulls came the sounds of wild life. A great owl hooted dismally. A fox yapped down by the stream bed, and again and again came the long-drawn howls of the wolf pack.

"They're running in closer tonight," Walter told himself. "I'm glad the Spirit Moose is hanging around close enough to be safe."

Finally he dozed off; and all at once it was morning.

"Before we go into breakfast," said Walter, as they dressed, "there's one matter I wish to talk over. Try to picture the men last night before and up to the time of that explosion. Who of our special suspects was in and who was out of the mess hall?"

"Terry," exclaimed Donald, "was in the whole time. Only he acted as though he had something on his mind."

"Right," agreed Clement. "And Johannes left early in the meal but came back promptly and remained."

"I agree," said Walter. "I'm noticing him all the time. As I recall, Rostinov came in late. Ole, I believe, was on deck the whole time but acting more sociable than usual."

"That is right," declared Raoul. "That leaves Jules Baladieu. Me, I think Jules finished rather early and left and did not come back. He leave, I think, with two or three others."

The other boys remembered a group leaving but were not sure about Jules.

"I'll keep a memorandum of these facts," said Walter. "They may help us later. Now for breakfast."

They found Doctor Maclaren awaiting them. He reported that Jean showed no change. "I shall stay with him today," said the physician, "going back tomorrow morning, if convenient."

"Better than today," laughed Walter, "both for the added period of your company and for Jean's sake." He grinned. "I might add, too, that the gale is still in full force."

"I am more than ever persuaded to remain for quieter weather," laughed the doctor.

Walter set his whole force at work that morning jerking out the scrambled pile of logs in the river bed and skidding them back to points on the slope above high water. The work was difficult and not lacking in danger. The cold was more extreme. The icy wind blew viciously down the stream channel. And the slopes were glare ice. Attempts to use the teams of horses were soon abandoned, for they were constantly falling. So the men handled the obstreperous timbers with cant-hooks and chains and ropes.

There was much complaining, some even among the most loyal men. Johannes growled steadily, and Rostinov proved a capable second. Ole worked sullenly. Jules's eyes sparked with anger, and he sputtered steadily to himself in French. But Walter ignored the grumblings and drove the force without ceasing. In this he was ably seconded by Black Mike, whom he was using in Jean's place. Both Walter and Black Mike not only directed the work but lent a hand continually in handling difficult timbers. Raoul, Clement, and Donald also plunged in and did what they could.

An open clash occurred before noon. Johannes, Terry, Owens, and Donald were handling a slightly twisted timber under Black Mike's direction. Terry and Donald were holding one end with their cant-hooks while Johannes and Owens were swinging the other end around. Suddenly Johannes appeared to slip on the frozen surface and bumped into Owens, upsetting him. At once Johannes let go his cant-hook, yelled, "Look out!" and leaped to one side.

The twisted log whipped around, skidding down on the fallen Owens, despite all Donald and Terry could do. Only Black Mike's instant action saved

Owens from terrible injury. As Johannes leaped aside, the dark, husky young fellow leaped by him, jabbed a boot through the ice crust and dropped down to catch the skidding log on his shoulder. The shock and pressing weight must have been tremendous. The blood rushed to Black Mike's face; the cords of his neck bulged. But he held back the log until Owens had rolled aside out of danger. Only then did he fling himself to one side. The great log jerked from Donald's and Terry's control and lunged, twisting and writhing, down the slope.

"*Timber-r-r-r!*" yelled Donald.

Men below leaped right and left or flung themselves headlong to escape the deadly monster, then sprang up to snarl oaths and hurl bitter invectives at the careless workers above.

Black Mike rose slowly and walked purposefully towards Johannes, who stood sullenly to one side. Not a word did Black Mike utter then, but as he reached the other man, his fist shot upward without warning and connected with Johannes's jaw. The terrific blow actually lifted the man from his feet and sent him crashing to the ground. He slid slowly downward until he spreadeagled and checked himself. With difficulty he staggered to his feet, shook his head to clear it, and with a bellow of rage, started back up the slope.

He had nearly reached the waiting Black Mike, when Walter, rushing across the slope, leaped between the two men. He waved back Black Mike with a gesture and a grin, then whipped around to face Johannes. Instantly the latter reached out a hand to shove Walter aside. Walter's own hand leaped out to grip the other's forearm. The grip tightened. Johannes screeched. He aimed a swinging blow at the young boss with his other fist. Walter ducked, but his grip tightened. Johannes went to his knees. Perspiration bedewed his forehead. He groaned.

"Had enough?" snapped Walter.

Johannes's pain-racked features quivered. He nodded.

Walter sprang aside and waited until Johannes had gotten to his feet and until others of the gang had gathered about. Then he turned to Black Mike.

"Sorry to interfere, Black Mike," he said clearly, so all could hear. "It was your affair. But I had a reason. Your quick thinking and courageous action saved serious injury, if not life. What was the trouble?"

Black Mike's eyes were red with anger. "He stumble against Owens and knock him down. Then he leap aside, the coward, and let that log roll down on a fallen man. I think he——"

"Looked like he knocked Owens over purposely," cried Donald.

Johannes's eyes shot sparks of anger. "*The kid lies!*" he shrieked, starting forward. But he brought up sharply as Walter's hand again darted forward.

"The kid calls them as he sees them," snapped Walter. "How about it, Terry?"

"I—I don't know, sir," said Terry, all the spirit out of him. He was surprisingly upset, his face haggard.

"What do you say, Black Mike?"

Black Mike's tones were thick with rage. "It look that way," he growled. "But as to his being a cow——"

"I slipped and fell against Owens," mouthed Johannes. "I didn't——"

"Johannes," snapped Walter, "you've been a trouble-maker ever since you set foot in camp. I've about made up my mind——"

"Boss—" Rostinov stepped close—"I know Johannes. We're what you call buddies. He did not mean trouble. Give him a chance."

"I'll give him a last chance," Walter rapped out sharply. "One more slip, understand, and out he goes, discredited for work in any camp."

"You mean blacklist?" Rostinov's tones were deadly; his eyes murderous.

Walter's glance locked with that of the other man, but he answered no word. For a long moment steady gray eyes stared, full and fearless, into those threatening black ones. Then the young boss turned on his heel and waved his men back to work. But as he passed Black Mike, he openly clapped him on the back. Under his breath he added the warning, "Watch your step! Someone may have it in for you now."

By early afternoon the log mass had been disentangled and all timbers had been moved back. Then Walter again sent the force into the field, despite grumbling at the cold and complaint of weariness from the hard work they had just completed.

"Too many smouldering fires," he said to Raoul. "If they sat around and grouched, there would be a half dozen mix-ups by night." He grinned. "I'm going to tire 'em out, and then Little John will ease their tempers with a special dinner."

"Me, I think you win," chuckled Raoul.

And so, for the moment, it appeared to be. The men tramped in wearily at dusk, to catch the fragrance of a meal that made their mouths water. And Little John and Spareribs served it with a sauce of quips and quarks and a pretended set-to between the two of them that had the gang roaring until the timbers shook.

From their end, Walter and his chums gazed interestedly down the board. Changes had taken place in the temper of that force that day. Walter wondered how far-reaching they would be. Respect had mounted in Black Mike's favor and in Walter's: that was clear. Johannes sat silent, practically sent to Coventry. Rostinov's eyes gleamed hotly as he stared about or talked with Ole and Jules. Terry sat sunk in thought. If an explosion were to come, it would come the sooner for the day's happenings.

"Why didn't you bounce that Johannes?" asked Donald later. "I know he did that purposely. And some of the men may think you weak."

"The worth-while men know better," put in Clement quickly.

"I don't want to break up that little group until I know what it's up to," said Walter. For a moment he looked very sober. "It's a big responsibility, fellows. I may be letting others in for trouble and danger. But Pete, down at Camp Seven, told me there is a trouble-making element at work. I want to get at its source. It may be here. And Dad, I know, has had threats." Beyond that he would say nothing, but more than one of the others suspected he knew more.

The next day again proved bitter. Doctor Maclaren reported that Jean was showing strength but had not yet come back to consciousness. "I can tell you just how to treat him, but I must go back this afternoon. I will return in a day or so, if necessary. Your man will probably recover. But when he regains his senses, do not disturb him with questions. The time will come for that later."

So that afternoon Walter again warmed up *Redbird* and prepared for his trip over the Carter Mountains. He and Clement both checked over the ship in every detail. Though neither said as much, each had in mind that some secret damage might have been done the craft. However, she appeared in perfect shape, and Walter took off neatly and shot away towards Wind Gap with his passenger.

About an hour later Clement heard the faint distant note of a plane and rushed out, thinking Walter had been forced to return. It proved, however, to be another biplane, flying very high. Its motor, he thought, either was not functioning perfectly or was dirty, for puffs of black smoke appeared at intervals.

Raoul, coming in later, mentioned seeing a few puffs of black smoke over near where the men were cutting, and Clement told him of the plane he had seen.

"Me, I think that plane must be from Oddie's camp. It must be the one I hear the other day. Oddie's son, he fly it, I hear."

Clement was busy that afternoon—at first with general account books, and then in the woods with a tally of timber cuts that Walter wished. This took him far afield, and finally to the very edge of the cutting. He was working here when the dulling light warned him that it was about time to turn back.

He had put up his notebook and was turning back when a flicker of movement at the foot of a slope caught his keen eyes. He stared sharply down and instantly realized that some person was in hiding down there. And instantly it came to mind: "The ski-runner!"

"I'll move casually around that way, as if coming into camp, and perhaps identify him," Clement told himself. "Then I'll hide and see who comes to meet him."

He moved down the slope, trying to appear as casual as possible. The stranger had faded into the cover of a spruce clump, so he swung nearer than he had first intended, thinking that he might execute a flank movement that would uncover him. In the eagerness of this chase no thought of fear occurred to him. He only regretted that The Black Shadow was not with him. In case of the man's flight, Lupus would have been of great assistance.

"Hands up!" The voice rasped behind him with startling suddenness. "Don't turn," it growled. "You're covered."

CHAPTER X
From Frying Pan Into Fire

CLEMENT STOPPED SHORT, HIS nerves jerking in surprise. Instinctively, despite the warning, he started to swing about. At once a stunning blow sent him crashing to the ground. For a period—how long he could not tell—he was conscious of nothing. Then his head cleared, quickly enough for him to think before he made a move. As a result, he made none for the moment. He found that he had been blindfolded; also that his hands had been fastened behind him.

But what really kept him motionless was the sound of voices near by. He wanted to hear all he could. The voices were kept low, and a bit disguised, he thought. One, he decided, was youthful; the other was that of a mature man.

"I tell you I don't want to do it," the younger was insisting. "It's kidnaping; and that's serious business."

"You're going to do it, and you're going to like it," growled the other.

"But I didn't agree to anything of this sort. All I wanted——"

"I know what you wanted," interrupted the older man. "And we'll make trouble, never fear. Only we'll carry your plan farther and make a killing, as well. You do your part and we'll be paying you."

"I don't want any money——"

"Suit yourself. But you do what we tell you. You're in as deep as we are. If we get into trouble, we'll see that you are in, too."

"But I'm afraid——" began the younger.

"Of course you are. You're yellow. But you take that chap to that little camp. Lock him in. Then, like as not, we've got the young boss where we want him. We c'n hold up Big Jim for a ransom for this kid. But the real prize package will be Big Jim's son. When the kid's missed, Walt will scatter his whole force to find a trail. Walt will probably go by himself or with one friend. We'll trail and hold him up; then pack him off to the hut and send Big Jim a notice. That Walt's been sticking too close to camp for us to lay hands on him, save when he's up in his plane."

"I tell you I won't," cried the young fellow. "No, no! Keep your hands off me. I—I—*let go!*" His voice rose to a shriek.

"Hush!" snarled the man viciously. "Either you take that chap to the hut now or I'll lay you out. *Quick!*"

"I'll take him," half groaned the younger man. "Only after this——"

"After this, we'll see," snarled the other. "But you fall down on any job of ours and you'll wish yourself dead. Now, stir that chap up and get going before anyone comes poking his nose down this way. Here, I'll rouse him."

Steps sounded, and a heavy foot thumped into Clement's side. He groaned and the man kicked again, growling, "Get up, you!"

Clement staggered to his feet and stood waveringly. He did not have to pretend in this. Being blindfolded and dizzy, he could hardly keep his feet. He was starting to protest when a gag was thrust in his mouth and made fast.

"Take his other arm," growled the older man, seizing Clement's right arm as he spoke. "Now, march him along. As soon as he gets his legs, I'll go back before I'm missed. March, you!" He shook his prisoner.

Clement marched, but he did it unsteadily, with a purpose. The more he delayed these two, the better. So he leaned first on one and then on the other and dragged his feet. And now and then he stamped one foot on the crust, mindful of the fact that signs like that would leave a trail for Walter or Raoul to follow. But the older man shook and threatened him, and so he had to be very careful.

He fell to counting his strides, presently, knowing that in that way he could roughly estimate the ground they covered. They had covered less than a mile, according to his reckoning, when the man on his right mumbled something and let go of him. Clement could hear his footsteps growing gradually fainter. The fellow was hastening back to camp.

"Come along easy," said the young fellow, putting an arm around him to steady him. "We don't aim to hurt you."

On they tramped, Clement delaying as much as he dared. But he could tell now that his present jailer was getting nervous and ugly in turn, and too much holding back would not be tolerated. They speeded up slightly, covering more than a mile before, from the continuous smooth surface, Clement realized they were on lake ice. Then they came up against a smooth body that towered high.

"Airplane," snapped the young fellow. "I'll boost you up. Reach up for a grip. That's it. Now, in you go. And I'll be right behind; so no monkey business."

Clement's spirits fell heavily. If he were transported by plane, all trace would be lost. And no knowing how far from camp he would be carried. Yet there was nothing he could do about it, save absorb all information possible. He could not even talk to the man who had charge of him.

Presently he felt himself being strapped in and extra wraps being placed about him. Then the motor roared. Shortly the plane took off. Clement tried to solve the direction from certain banks and turns, but soon gave that up as an impossible job for one of his slight flying experience.

But one idea did occur to him, and he acted upon it at once. His blindfold! If he could loosen it so as to get even a peek, he might locate some landmark. Of course, he had flown over all this region the previous summer. And though winter views were bound to appear very different, there was a chance of his recognizing where he was.

He began by working his facial muscles. Also he settled lower in his seat, as if striving to get out of the cutting wind. Presently, with the utmost care, he began rubbing one side of his head against an edge of the cockpit. For some time he appeared to be getting nowhere; that blind had been skilfully applied. But at long last he felt it give ever so slightly. He redoubled his efforts. If only he could get one eye free!

The plane was banking sharply, and instinct told Clement the time for landing had come. He made a last desperate effort, and one eye came partially clear. He saw a long and rather narrow frozen lake surface beneath him towards which they were rapidly descending. He did not recognize it. Then he looked off; and there was something he did know. It was the distant peak of Grand Dome Mountain. He saw also an outjutting ridge and on it a towering black mark. That was, he knew, the fire tower from which the boys had kept guard over the Northrop forest holdings the summer before.

Now they were dropping rapidly. The lake surface rose to meet them. A swaying jolt, and the landing had been made. The plane shot on. But Clement noticed little now. He was trying to fix clearly in mind the angle of direction of Grand Dome from the lake. Should a chance of escape offer, he would know how to locate himself.

The plane slowed to a halt. Clement debated whether to try to shift that blindfold up again, so his guard would not know that he had looked off, or to wait and attempt to get a glimpse of the young man behind him. But the matter was not left to him to decide. Hands reached by his head and jerked the blindfold up.

"I saw you working on that," snapped the young man. "Let it alone or it will be the worse for you. Do as you're told and you won't be hurt. Now, stand up and I'll help you out."

That was accomplished with some difficulty, for Clement's hands were still bound. He toppled rather heavily to the ice. Then his companion pulled him to his feet and, keeping a tight grip on one arm, directed his course across the ice and then for a short distance through a woods trail. That it was overgrown, or was no regular trail, Clement was sure, for branches of fir slapped his face or brushed heavily against his body. He caught the rich fragrance of spruce trees.

All at once he was halted. A lock rasped in an icy padlock. A door grated, and he was forced into a hut. Evidently a two-room affair, at least, he realized, for he was propelled across a rough floor and through another doorway and pushed onto a bench.

"Sit there!" snapped his guard.

Other sounds succeeded. The man moved back and forth, in and out. There were thumps as he brought in and threw down armfuls of wood. Finally the man ordered him to stand. Then he released the bound hands.

"You are to make no move," he directed, "until you hear the door close be-hind me. Then you may remove the blindfold and make yourself comfortable. Let me go through your pockets." He did that expertly. "I'm keeping your knife and I'm taking the ax in your belt. You will find fuel ready and matches on a table. Also provisions. But I warn you not to try to escape. You can't make it. Besides, you are in absolute wilderness, miles on miles from any camp. So take things easy."

The man left the room, slamming the door after him. A lock clicked, and a wooden bar thumped into place. The outer door banged, and there followed the sound of boots crunching through snow crust. Still Clement waited. And then he heard the ship taking off.

For a few minutes Clement found himself forced to massage his hands to restore the circulation. Finally, however, he was able to tear the bandanna from his eyes and remove the painful gag. He found himself stiff and sore and thoroughly chilled. And the air of that room was Arctic in temperature. A fire came first.

With stiffened fingers he groped for his own matchbox, and after breaking half his matches, managed to light one. That sufficed to locate a little drum stove with twigs for kindling and a loose pile of stove wood. With consider-able difficulty, he managed to get a fire going and also to light a candle that was stuck in a bottle on the table.

His first glance, as he stamped about to keep himself warm, showed that the place was intended for a prisoner. The walls were of heavy logs. The door was of double planking with concealed hinges. The window was heavily barred with log sections. It was also concealed by a close-growing spruce thicket, so practically no light filtered through. For the rest there were the light table and a built-in bunk. There was no chimney, a stovepipe leading up through a heavy roof.

"Looks like that chap was right," Clement told himself. "I can't escape. But that doesn't mean I won't be freed in short order, once the camp crowd really gets to work. Meanwhile, I expect a good meal won't do me any harm."

He searched a cupboard and found canned and other package goods from which to make a selection. A few cooking utensils were also available. So it was but the work of a few minutes to heat some soup and to follow this with hot baked beans and fancy crackers. He ate leisurely and found himself feeling much refreshed. He even felt rather cheerful. He might have to wait over the next day or so before he was discovered. But it was all in the nature of an adventure.

A little later, however, as he lay resting in his bunk recalling his experience step by step, uneasiness began to creep in. His disappearance would cause considerable anxiety to his friends; and the search would take men from work. Then, as he thought on, he began to worry about Walter. He had not thought much about the threat against Walter at the time. Now it came back: this gang had it in mind to kidnap Big Jim's son and hold him for heavy ransom. And he, Clement, was to be the bait to pull Walter away from his companions sufficiently to make possible his capture.

Here was something else again. After all, it would not do to lie back and wait for rescue; he might simply find himself still in captivity with Walter as a companion. Walter must be warned.

"I've *got* to find a way to get out," Clement muttered.

He jumped to his feet and began another search of his quarters. This disclosed, however, no new way of escape. He looked around for something with which he might batter a way out. But the only thing that caught his eye was a small and light poker. It would bend he knew at the first attempt to pry anything loose with it.

Discouraged, he lay back on the bunk once more, to try to think things out. Oddly that poker kept coming to his mind. How could he use it? There ought to be some way.

Suddenly he sat up with shining eyes. "I have it! I'm not likely to be disturbed; at least, not until late tonight, when one of the gang from camp may work over. There'll be time. Let's see, it's bright moonlight, though the moon rises late. And I have the angle towards Grand Dome. I can tramp that way until I strike the camp trail; then follow that in. It won't be so terribly long a distance. That flyer must have simply circled about to confuse me. Now, to work!"

Eagerly he stirred up the coals in the little drum stove, stoked with the best wood he could pick out, and then thrust the end of the poker in the hottest section. While it was heating, he set about refilling his matchbox and preparing a lunch to take with him. For now he was so determined to get out that he was sure he would.

The minute the poker was red-hot he began burning into the wood of the door around the lock. He made barely a faint groove before the poker had cooled. While it was re-heating, he dug at the groove with an old kitchen knife that had been left him. Alternating with red-hot poker and knife, he dug on. It was desperately slow work. More than that, he was not sure, even if the lock finally gave, that he could manage about the outside bar. He dared not let himself think about that.

More than two hours later his poker had burnt openings on two sides of the lock. Before going farther, he stuck the poker through a cut and prodded upward until finally its point touched the bar. He shoved. The bar gave. With a thrill of joy, he realized it was set in open angle irons. He shoved harder. The bar raised higher. But he experienced many failures before, at long last, the bar slipped over and clattered to the floor.

"Now I'll be out in a jiffy," he exclaimed.

Springing over to the pile of firewood, he selected two pieces. One he pressed against the weakened lock. The other he used as a hammer with which to pound upon it. But the lock would not yield, and he was reduced to the slow cutting with the hot poker. Another long hour of labor followed. Then, at last, the lock yielded and the door swung open.

Swiftly Clement drew on his heavy Mackinaw and passed into the outer and unheated room. To his delight he found a large ax, as well as his own little camp ax. He restored the latter to his belt and with the other directed a few husky blows at the outer door that quickly broke the lock. He was free!

Clement stole a glance at his watch. "Well on towards ten o'clock," he muttered. "I must hustle. But every minute will bring me nearer to camp and so to some search party."

Picking up his lunch, he put out the candle, closed the inner door and the outer as well, and stood outside in the bitter cold. The sky was clear, and the rising moon, reflecting from the snow, gave light in abundance. Swiftly he moved through the little thicket in which the hut had been cleverly concealed and came out on the edge of the lake surface. It stretched on before him, long and narrow. And far beyond, above the forest growth, glittered the summit of Grand Dome.

"This is West Finger Lake," he told himself. "I remember its shape. I'll go straight across and then through the woods towards Grand Dome until I hit the blazed trail. Got to watch sharp in order not to overrun it. Then I'll turn right on the trail. Means ten miles at the very least. Here goes."

He sped lightly down the frozen surface of the lake, anxious to cover ground as rapidly as possible. But in the bitter air, his wind gave out and he slowed down. Thereafter he forced himself to a more leisurely pace.

After a couple of miles of easy travel he reached the end of the lake and was forced to plunge into the woods. At once the going became decidedly more difficult. There was much underbrush through this section, some windfalls, and not a few boulders. He felt wearied before he had gone a mile. More than that, after a little he had to stop continually to examine trees right and left for the telltale blazes that would show him he had struck the trail. This search was made the more difficult because of ice and frozen snow that still adhered to many trunks.

He had about decided he had overrun the trail and must either go back and search for it or else strike out for camp without regard to it, when he saw a tree blaze. His heart leaped in relief. At least the going would be easier. He swung right and speeded up. It was already nearly one o'clock.

Thus far, he had been intent only on getting across to the trail. Now, as he sped along the route towards camp, he began to give ear and eye to sights and sounds. Even in the moonlight, he could pick up certain animal tracks—of deer and moose especially. Once a great horned owl screamed and choked dismally down trail. *How-O! How-O! Hoo-hoo-hoo-hoo!* And a little later he made out its shadowy figure flying silently away. A fox barked. As he passed a thicket he caught the hoarse wuffle of a moose.

And then, all without warning, far to his right the wolf pack broke into full cry. For the first time since the moment of his capture, a shiver of uneasiness and fear rippled up his spine. He had not thought of the wolves. Now he realized that he had no weapon with which to fight them off, and that the cold was too bitter for him to safely roost many hours in a tree.

Instinctively he loosened the little ax in his belt. It was of no value, he knew, for direct defense if attacked. But already one plan had come to him. If cornered, he might have time to build a fire and hold off the pack until daylight or until rescued. The ax would help in that. In fact, he used it almost immediately to cut some strips of dry birchbark and a couple of pine knots. These he carried along with him.

Now he moved with all the speed he dared. If he were cornered, it might mean failure to get warning to Walter in time. That, he felt, was all important. But as he ran stumblingly along the snow-covered trail, he had an ear ever to the wolves. The pack was hot on a trail, still to his right. But it was edging slowly towards him. He slowed down, hoping pursued and pursuers would cross the Grand Dome trail well ahead of him. The din increased, died away, broke out again. He stopped beside a tangle of windfalls.

Suddenly, with a start, he saw something shadowy speed by on his right, going with long graceful bounds. He realized it was a buck deer. As he watched, it paralleled his trail for a ways, then turned and crossed it some distance to his rear.

Tense, uneasy, he waited. This might or might not be the quarry of the vicious timber wolves. Then all doubt was laid at rest. Across a little open glade he saw two dark figures, flying along, bodies close to the ground. They were running parallel, a little distance apart—the hunting leaders of the pack. And behind them came a terrifying number of other racing figures—at least twenty.

The instant they had passed far enough for his movement not to attract attention, Clement sped at top speed along the trail towards camp. More than once he took sharp headers, but picked himself up and ran pantingly on. Every second counted. Behind him he heard a terrifying chorus of yelps and snarls, and he knew the quarry was down. He drew on his reserves and sprinted on.

And then he heard it—a long-drawn signal howl, directly back along his freshly made trail. He heard other wolves give cry. The snarling and yelping decreased. The hunting cries deepened. His time of trial had come. With fingers that trembled, but with lips set firmly, he struck his matches and touched off the bark he carried. As the flame mounted, he fashioned his torch and waved it until the flame grew vigorous. Then he looked around. Altogether too near for comfort, several gray forms sat or stood on the snow, the torchlight reflecting from their yellow-green eyes. And he saw other ugly figures stealing off to left and right. In a moment the circle about him would have been formed.

CHAPTER XI
Indian Pete to the Rescue

CLEMENT HAD BEEN IN more than one tight place before and had kept his nerve. But never had he felt the threat of deadly danger as he did now. There was menace in every move of the snarling beasts as they sat around or skulked about or made tentative rushes in his direction. Their rolled-back lips showed vicious fangs. The mouths of some dripped blood from their recent kill. Their greenish-amber eyes, as they reflected the torchlight, burned with a savage hunt lust.

Even as Clement gazed about, the circle closed around him. That doubled his anxiety. He could not look in all directions at once. As he slowly revolved, keeping eye on each little group in turn, he fought against the feeling that always the wolves for the moment behind him were edging nearer, closing in—closing in.

The temptation to climb the nearest tree available, before action started, was almost irresistible. Yet even as he looked about for one that could be climbed swiftly and easily, Clement found himself fighting back that urge. He told himself that the cold was intense and would increase each hour. However thick his wraps, he would freeze to death if perched in a tree all night. Only in motion was there safety—in motion or a fire.

Motion, yes! There was that other vital motive to drive him on. If Walter were back from his flight in *Redbird*, he would surely be leading the search by now. And on his trail would be the members of the gang detailed to capture him. Walter—on guard—might not be easily taken. But Walter, with all thought for his chum, might be taken by surprise. He must be warned.

So Clement already knew he must go on—on as long as that was possible. Then, if forced to halt, he must stop at a point where he could build a fire, for in fire was a certain safety, both from wolves and cold. This made him think of his torch, and at once a new anxiety beset him. It was burning up too fast. He must get more material without delay.

Slowly he swung about on his heels. The wolves ranged from forty to fifty feet away, heads all his way, expectantly.

"Looks like the first move is mine," said Clement, talking to keep up his courage. "I appear to be—" he chuckled—"a movable feast." He forced a grin and felt better.

Slowly he moved a few feet towards camp, waving his torch and keeping it in a bright glow. The wolves ahead snarled and gave way grudgingly. Those behind crept after him, edging slightly closer. That fiery, sparking thing in his hands kept them uneasy. But for how long?

Presently he came to a small dead pine. It was not of a kind to give him torch material. But another use occurred to him. He applied his torch, and the powdery dry growth exploded into flame. As the tongues of flame shot upward and a sharp crackling sounded the wolves drew away in evident alarm.

Clement hurried on. When he glanced back a moment later, the wolves to the rear were circling around the flaming tree and coming on, and those nearer were again closing in ahead. These latter, too, were now more stubborn, less inclined to give ground as he continued his steady advance. There was more threat, too, in their snarls and short rushes.

Unexpectedly he spotted something, just off the trail, that gave him instant relief. It was a dry dead birch, probably toppled over in the recent gale. Swiftly he made his way to it and set his torch in a crotch. Then, with the aid of his camp ax, he began stripping off great layers of bark.

Busy at this work, he failed to notice that the torch flame gradually lessened and that the wolves were crowding closer. Only just in time, out of the corners of his eyes, did he catch the motion of the more determined pack leader as it flung itself towards him in a headlong rush. Instantly he snatched the torch, brought it around in a sweeping arc that made it glow afresh, and jammed its flaming tip square in the face of the vicious beast as it rose in a final spring. This deflected its charge. It yelped in pain and terror, rolled over and over, and scurried away. At once Clement swung about to meet the certain threat of the other leader. At once it backed away.

Making up a fresh torch roll of the bark he had stripped, Clement fired it. Then he gathered up a reserve supply under his free arm and once more started along the trail. But now the wolves in front held their ground more and more stubbornly, yielding only when he was almost upon them.

"Get back, you chaps!" snapped Clement sharply, more to steady himself than for any other purpose. But seeing that the pack stirred uneasily at the sound of his voice, he went on talking. "I don't like your looks. No, I've no desire for closer acquaintance. Keep your distance."

Still, though some wolves withdrew a few steps, the pack leaders continued their tentative rushes, mere threats as yet. Despite his ignorance of the ways of wolves, Clement could not doubt that they were nerving themselves for a real dash at the feared human within their death circle.

Yet, with that threat facing him, Clement laughed aloud. An idea had occurred to him. It might work—work long enough for him to gain a little more distance along the trail, and perhaps replenish his fuel supply or find a shelter point. He cleared his throat and tested his voice, at the same time thrusting his torch at a gray beast that charged in too close for comfort.

"Look out, you beast! *Scat!!* Away with you!!!" The voice came from behind the wolf leader. It leaped a couple of feet to one side and whirled around. Other wolves leaped aside. Uneasiness prevailed around half the circle, "On your toes! March!!" whipped sharp tones back of the forward wolves. They, too, shifted and whirled about as Clement moved swiftly forward.

"I never expected to try my ventriloquism on you chaps," laughed Clement, determined to keep talking. He began to play his voice about, here and there—often in the very ear of a wolf—as he moved on. But all the time he was shooting glances around, selecting trees to climb, if forced to that act; looking for fuel for torches or night fire, if that were possible as an alternate. Yet constantly his eyes strayed about that tightening circle. It would not do to be off guard for an instant.

Slowly, now, he pressed on. His voice had become hoarse from the unnatural use. The wolves were getting used to the mysterious tones. He could sense their temper. And, for a moment, he was distant from any tree he could climb in a hurry. Another rush started, and stopped a dozen feet away. The more courageous leader launched himself full tilt. Clement backed against a tree and set himself to jab with his torch and strike with his ax. The wolf rose high in a magnificent leap——

Cra-ack!

The sharp report seemed to split the air. In mid-leap the great wolf shook convulsively and collapsed. Clement swung around to find the other leader in full charge and the whole pack in motion. Again a shot rang out, and the charging wolf turned several somersaults. Clement sprang aside as the snarling pack leaped upon the fallen leaders. For the moment he was forgotten. He backed off watchfully along the trail. Still again the rifle spoke. This time many of the wolves sprang for cover.

"Go to camp," ordered a guttural voice. "Indian Pete stands wolves off."

His limbs suddenly all a-tremble, Clement staggered away without a word. Some yards farther on he looked back and made out in the moonlight the tall and magnificently erect figure of the Indian guide and runner of the Northrop Camps. The man was facing towards the wolves. In fact, his rifle again belched fire at the instant. Then the Indian turned and waved him on. He obeyed, while from behind sounded yelps and snarls and vicious mouthings.

For a little time he tramped rapidly on. Then, without consciousness of any sound, he realized the Indian was close behind. Even then, Clement remembered to keep quiet for a brief space. At long last he said over his shoulder, "Indian Pete came at the right time. His rifle spoke at the exact instant of great need. It did not miss."

Silence fell again. Only after quite an interval did there come a reply in guttural tones. "Many moons ago Indian Pete say this young man have power and will to learn. He have learn. Indian Pete saw him fool the wolves. He heard the magic of his voice that flies about like a bird. The young man makes great magic."

"Say," exclaimed Clement, forgetting dignity in his surprise, "how long have you been watching?"

"Indian Pete has been ready to act for some time. Danger came only in the last minute."

They went on in dignified silence for a space, broken at last by the Indian. "Indian Pete," he went on, speaking in the third person as he often did, "has questions in his mind to which he does not see the answers. Why does the young man travel alone, at this hour and in this cold? He carries no arms. Why did he not climb a tree or build him a fire? Great need must press."

"Indian Pete is right," said Clement, after a suitable interval. "Great need presses. I have been a prisoner. I broke loose to make camp and warn Big Jim's son that traitors are in his force. They seek this night to make him prisoner while he searches for me. My feet must be swift to reach him."

"The young man is weary," answered the Indian. "Indian Pete will go ahead, will seek out Big Jim's son, and will see that no harm comes to him. The young man will keep the rifle."

"We go together," insisted Clement. "Wolves still trail." He pointed to a shadowy figure skulking to one side. "Without a weapon, Indian Pete might find himself in just such danger as mine."

"The young man with the voice of magic has eyes that can see," complimented the Indian. "Indian Pete will lead. The young man will follow in his footsteps. Three shots will tell that he is coming." He lifted his rifle and punctured the air with three evenly spaced reports.

They moved on swiftly and wordlessly. They were now only two or three miles out. Suddenly a wolfish shadow sped like a streak across his trail. Indian Pete half lifted his rifle; then he let it drop into the hollow of his arm. The creature flew on. The next instant a wild yelp, half of terror, broke from a skulking wolf on the right. Two clawing, biting, snarling creatures rolled and tumbled into the open. Then they broke apart—one fleeing, the other pursuing.

A shrill reedy whistle pierced the air. The pursuing animal halted almost in mid-stride, swung about, and came swiftly towards Clement.

"The Black Shadow," cried Clement. "Here, Lupus! Indian Pete, Raoul must be close."

"He comes from the left," responded Indian Pete quietly.

The great wolf dog rubbed up against Clement affectionately. After thus greeting him and submitting to an instant's petting, the big fellow went over to the Indian. The latter laid a hand on the big, handsome head. For an instant Clement thought the Indian's grave expression was actually going to yield to an amused smile, at his own earlier belief that Lupus was a spirit.

"The Spirit Wolf!" said the man. "Big Jim's son was right."

From the left Clement made out now the slender figure of Raoul. The French Canadian saluted the Indian gravely and in simple terms, but his two hands went out impulsively to Clement.

"Me, I am now happy!" he said.

But Clement had other matters much on his mind. "Where is Walt?" he demanded.

"He search to the right," said Raoul, "just on chance. He think you were taken away in a plane."

"I was," snapped Clement. "But, Raoul, he must be warned at once." In the fewest possible words he summed up the situation. "How can we best reach him?"

"Me, I'll send Lupus," exclaimed Raoul instantly. With a snap of his fingers he caught the great dog's attention. "Find Walt, Lupus!" He waved his hand towards the right. "Guard him! Go!!"

At the last word the wolf dog leaped away and began coursing back and forth. In a minute he was gone from sight.

"Now, what should _we_ do?" demanded Clement.

"Big Jim's son," said the tall guide, "knows Indian Pete's rifle. He hear the shots and come. Just ahead, on an open ridge, all wait."

"Won't the wolf pack make trouble for him?" questioned Clement uneasily.

"Walter is armed," said Raoul.

"The wolves hunt to the north," added Indian Pete. The faintest suggestion of a grin broke his solemn expression. "By now they know many men to be this way; and strange things have happened to them around here."

He turned and led the way along the trail, coming presently to the crown of a gradual slope, largely bare of tree growth, save for scattering clumps of fir balsam. Here he stopped and fired three spaced shots. And Clement, noticing closely now, realized that the long-barreled piece had its own particular note.

Time passed. The cold bit deep. Across the open space, far below, the silhouette of a deer flitted gracefully, but with astonishing speed, from cover to cover. Then the shadowy figure of a man detached itself from the far cover and started for the foot of the slope.

"Me, I think that is Walter," exclaimed Raoul.

"I'll give him a call," exclaimed Clement.

"*Silence!*" hissed the Indian.

The others looked around at him in surprise. He was crouching low and fading back into cover. As he went he signaled them to remain where they were. Even as they stared after him, he vanished.

"What's up now?" murmured Clement uneasily.

Raoul clutched his arm and pointed towards a clump of firs towards which the solitary figure was advancing. A bit of shadow appeared to move. Moonlight glittered on some object. An armed man stood there.

Clement gasped. But even as he hesitated, on the verge of disobeying Indian Pete's injunction, a racing shadow leaped from the woods and tore, with a yelp of greeting that reached even to the young men on the ridge, straight for the figure in the open. No questions about the two being Walter and Lupus!

Almost at once, however, the leaping dog stiffened, facing towards the thicket. The watchers saw Walter swing partly about and jerk his rifle up, ready for action. And they saw the ambushed figure crouch and fade from view. Instinctively they started forward down the slope. But they had barely taken a half dozen strides when several other men broke from another point and came forward, calling to Walter, who waved a hand and answered. The two groups joined and came on.

"Indian Pete, he spot that man and trail him," said Raoul, as they moved on, now, down the slope.

Clement broke into a run and, below them, Walter did the same. The two chums met and clasped hands. Walter wasted no words.

"Held up and taken off in a ship?" he asked.

"Yes," said Clement. "I escaped later."

"Tell just the bare facts to the men," directed Walter.

"A man was in that clump of trees preparing to hold you up," went on Clement. "He was scared when the others broke cover. Indian Pete is after him."

"Keep quiet about that," said Walter. "Lupus warned me that something was up. Now meet the men."

A half dozen men, led by Black Mike, were now drawing near and yelling greetings. Clement felt a warm thrill at the friendliness of that reception. Even Terry was cordial. Clement stated the main facts of his capture and merely said he had gotten away after his guard had left. All moved on in a group, talking excitedly, heading for camp. Indian Pete had not reappeared.

They were within a mile of camp when from ahead came the wild clangor of the camp triangle, beaten steadily and with mighty strokes.

"Word's gotten in that the lost is found," chuckled a woodsman, "and Little John is celebrating."

But Walter looked serious. "It may be trouble," he said anxiously. "Isn't that a glow of light ahead?"

"*Fire!*" cried Black Mike and broke into a run.

Tired as all were, a mad race began, while ahead of them the triangle kept up its warning and steadily the glow deepened.

"A camp building," panted Clement, running beside Walter.

"Too far to the right," puffed Walter, "to be a main camp!"

The leading man topped a slight rise. "*The hangar!*" he yelled.

The others gained the ridge, and the scene lay before them. The little hangar was well ablaze. In its light a few black dots of men could be seen, evidently chopping through the ice to get water. The men from the woods lunged downward while ahead the flames mounted higher.

Boom!

The heavy explosion shook the ground. Sheets of flame broke through the building. Another explosion followed. The roof went up, and blazing embers showered the men fleeing from the neighborhood of the building.

Walter slowed down. "The end of *Redbird!*" he gasped.

CHAPTER XII
Swapping Ideas

IMMEDIATELY, HOWEVER, WALTER LUNGED forward once more, calling over his shoulder, "Clem, better turn in at once. I'm going down to see if I can locate any clues. That place was set afire, without any doubt."

"I'll go too," declared Clement. "Time enough to rest, later."

They sped on down the slope and over the ice to the hangar. This was now all ablaze. Many parts were falling in. So hopeless was any attempt to save anything that the men had let up their efforts to break through the thick lake ice to get water.

"We'll start bucket lines, just the same, Black Mike," called Walter. "May be some signs of the persons responsible," he added in a lower tone.

Black Mike nodded and ran over to the men. Again axes began cutting into the ice; and soon two lines of men were passing buckets of water to head men who dashed the contents on the structure. Gradually they fought their way in. But gray dawn had fully come before the last embers had sizzled out. There remained only a motor and some other twisted metal and small heaps of blackened fragments.

It was only when the excitement was almost at an end that a scorched and blackened figure rushed over to Clement and thrust out both hands to grasp his and wring them.

"*Geewillikers!*" came in Donald's voice, hoarse with smoke and excitement. "What happened? Where have you been? Who found you? What——"

"Lay off, Don!" chuckled Clement wearily. "Is that really you? You look like the end man in an impromptu minstrel show. I'll tell you the whole story later."

"Well, I haven't been idle myself," grinned Donald. The grin faded abruptly as his lips cracked. "I was the first to see the fire and give the alarm. But there were too few men around camp, and she blazed up too fast for anything to be done."

"Who was the first to reach the hangar?" asked Walter.

"I was," exclaimed Donald. "I knew where your reserve key was. So I got it while Little John was punishing that triangle. And believe me, I flew down. I took that slope in a hop, three skids, a tumble, and a nose slide. I thought, you know, there might be time to get *Redbird* out. But there wasn't a chance. She was ablaze. I was sort of afraid her tank would blow before I got a look around. The place was rank with the smell of gasoline. It must have been poured from one of the metal containers. Just as the flames drove me out, I saw that two or three boards had been pried off the side of the hangar away from camp."

"You took too much chance, playing around with fire and gasoline ready to mix it up," said Walter. "This thing is my fault. I should have had a watch kept over this place."

"It's my fault," retorted Clement. "If I had not let myself be captured, it wouldn't have happened. The plane was fired to prevent you, Walt, from trying to trace the plane that took me away."

"*Gee!*" yelled Donald excitedly. "Were you really kidnapped, Clem?"

"We'll talk adventures after we've had some rest," said Walter. He beckoned to Raoul to join them. "You chaps are not to speak of the fact that Indian Pete is about. He may have reasons for keeping in the background. In fact, for the present, say as little as possible about anything that happened tonight." He grinned and added, "But listen with both ears."

As all nodded, Donald broke out again, "I've one more thing to say right now, though. I found a pocketknife with one broken blade. It lay beside the plane and had evidently been used in ripping up things about the plane before setting her ablaze."

"Good!" laughed Walter. "Our famous detective is at work. Now I'll do my part. I wish to see if I can trail the chap who came to the back of the hangar. You fellows turn in and rest. No work today until afternoon."

"You're not going to do that trailing alone," exclaimed Clement uneasily.

"Me, I will go with him, and Lupus too," said Raoul quickly.

"I don't intend to be babied," snapped Walter crossly.

Raoul chuckled and clapped him on the back. Presently they moved away, deep in some discussion. Clement and Donald turned back and scrambled up the slippery slope to their own camp, the latter still striving to choke down the flood of questions that filled his eager mind. They had hardly entered their little hut when the door opened silently behind them. Donald gave a gasp of surprise as a tall figure slipped in. Then he grinned a welcome as he recognized Indian Pete. The guide looked half frozen and very weary. Without a word he moved to the drum stove and crouched over it.

"Big Jim's son will be here shortly," said Clement.

The Indian grunted.

"Shall I get you food?" Clement asked.

"Indian Pete does not wish it known he is here," said the guide.

"I've a lunch I fixed up before leaving the hut where I was imprisoned," exclaimed Clement. He dug it out of his coat and held it out. "It's better than nothing."

"Enough!" said the Indian. He took it and gulped it down hungrily.

He had barely finished the last crumb when Walter and Raoul entered and greeted him warmly. At once the Indian took a letter from within his deerskin jacket and gave it to the young boss. "Big Jim say to give to his son when no man save these young men see."

"It is well," said Walter. He waited a moment. "What of the man whom you trailed this night?"

The Indian shrugged his shoulders. "Indian Pete see the man in ambush when Big Jim's son come into the open. He circle to capture the man. But the man hear others come, and he go quietly. The hard crust left little mark. Big Jim's son must watch. His enemy has a long stride. The span of a hand longer than a tall man. The right boot heel, it wears more than the left. And this—" he passed over a shred of cloth—"is from his coat where he stand in hiding. Indian Pete go on and study the trail of the two men who take prisoner the young man with the magic voice. Your enemy was not one of those two."

"What's this about a magic voice?" exclaimed Donald. "Say, Clem, did you charm your keeper and get away by that means?"

"Indian Pete knows that the young man will not tell his own story," said the guide. "But the story of how he talked into the ears of the wolves must be told. Listen!"

Simply, dramatically, with many striking gestures, Indian Pete pictured for the others what he himself had seen, holding his little audience spellbound. And after that, under a storm of questioning, Clement was forced to fill in with the details of the remainder of his trip.

"*Geewillikers!*" exploded Donald once more, his eyes big and round. "I'll say that was an adventure!"

"And a great risk to take for my sake, Clem," said Walter soberly. "I shall not forget it." He turned to the guide. "You must have come through West Cut, to have been on hand when needed. And one takes that trail only to save time. Does that mean you cannot stay here? I could use your skill——"

"Indian Pete travels again after an hour's rest," said the Indian. "Ice has brought down the singing wires that carry messages. Big Jim say messages must go."

"Then rest in that bunk," said Walter, "and go with our thanks when the time comes. We will all turn in."

When the others roused from deep sleep to the clang of hammer on triangle, they found that the signal was not for breakfast but for dinner. Indian

Pete was gone. Walter sat, fully dressed, reading the communications the guide had brought. His expression was very sober. Outside, the weather was gloomy, too. There was an effect of fog, but a second glance showed that a fine needle-like snow was falling.

"By gar!" exclaimed Little John, when the young fellows tramped in. "They spring ze trap, but Clem, he no fool bird to be caught that way. By gar! Wait until I get my hands on those chaps. Hunh?"

Walter grinned as the cook shook his enormous fists at imaginary enemies. But he sobered instantly. "What about the weather, Little John?"

The cook stepped to a window and stared out. He spat disgustedly and threw up his hands. "By *gar*! She snow again. Another blizzard! In five-six hour she hit hard."

"I thought so," said Walter uneasily. He sat silent during the meal, eating little. At its close he rose and told the men that work would be pressed that afternoon. "We are behind in output," he ended, "and we are sure to lose more time in the storm now coming."

"It's already too much of a storm for outside work," growled Johannes.

"By gar!" chuckled Little John. His high laugh rippled teasingly as he eyed the glowering man. "She have fear, this leetle man, that the cold will hurt heem. Never mind, Monsieur Johannes——" he bowed low with hands outspread—"Leetle John, he will have a warm supper, hot milk——"

"*Stow that!*" flared Johannes, leaping to his feet, while the men shouted.

Little John, however, simply laughed again until his body was aquiver, while Spareribs accompanied him with a deep bass "Haw—haw—haw!" Johannes, muttering threats, stamped noisily from the room, followed by the laughing men.

"Good for the cook!" said Walter softly. "He nipped complaint in the bud. Raoul, I'll want you in the field to help keep the men pepped up. Clem, you and Don scale all timber—birch, oak, and hickory—that we have on the runways. All you can get is a rough estimate. I need it quick. We can talk later, fellows. From the looks of things we'll have time to sit around and talk tomorrow."

That proved a difficult afternoon. The men trudged out in the face of a bitter wind that sand-papered exposed flesh with needle snow. And steadily wind and cold increased and snow thickened. Constant oversight was necessary to keep things moving at all. Black Mike directed felling and sawing. Walter oversaw the skidding of the timbers out of the woods. Raoul watched the stacking at the rollways.

Yet things moved slowly. Some men started loafing, and that habit proved contagious. Black Mike stormed at his men, driving them with a hard rein and whip. The sulky Ole, rebuked for gross carelessness in felling a tree so that it lodged badly against another, swung a mighty fist at Black Mike. Black Mike retaliated with a blow that landed Ole ten feet away. Yet Black Mike was learning. His old-time sullenness had left him. Now and then he gave gruff praise.

Raoul urged and praised his men. Walter jollied his workers while retaining a certain firmness. In general, he kept the logs moving out steadily to the rollways. Only now and then did some driver manage to throw a timber against a standing tree or drop it in some awkward position that required the help of extra men and teams to free it.

Many of the troubles of the afternoon were due to straight carelessness and indifference. But some, Walter was sure, were intended. Yet so cleverly were things done that it was almost impossible to pin definite acts of insubordination against anyone. Yet before the afternoon was over the young boss was satisfied that trouble was centering around the men he had under suspicion.

Steadily the wind mounted and the snow fell thicker. By the time work was called off, a full gale was blowing and drifts were forming rapidly. The men stumbled in, numb with cold and in an ugly frame of mind.

Once back in the warm camp buildings, however, they threw off their grouches, knowing full well that they would have a holiday on the morrow. At their meal, for once they ate leisurely, roaring with laughter as they fenced with Little John.

Later, in the Men's Camp, an impromptu entertainment took form. Walter left early, but his chums stayed and took part in the program before drifting out, one by one. Raoul gave a skilful rendering of several magician's tricks he had picked up. Clement sent his magic voice flitting here and there. Donald put Skipper through his latest tricks. One by one, as they finished, they slipped out and joined Walter in their own hut.

"Now," said Walter, when they were all together, "we'll begin by having Clem give a detailed account of his experience. And no holding back, Clem! This is another hold-up. We're going to strip you clean of every fact."

Coloring painfully, at times, under the necessity of going into details over his own actions, Clement obeyed. He started with his first glimpse of the figure hiding just outside the camp, of his own stalking, and the unexpected attack that laid him out.

"Did you get a line on your assailant?" asked Walter.

"I was blindfolded. I think he was the older man of the two. He must have been the one who came to meet the skulker. The skulker must have been the flyer who took me off; and he was younger."

"I wonder how they make their appointments," went on Walter. "In such a vicious winter as this, they would hardly arrange at one meeting a time for the next, at least with any hope of keeping it."

"I can make a guess," responded Clement. "Yesterday a plane came over, high up. It appeared to have a dirty motor. It let off five puffs of black smoke. Later Raoul spoke of seeing smoke puffs on the edge of camp, not from the plane. Why not smoke signals—five puffs, five o'clock? That was about the time."

"Sounds reasonable," said Walter. "I think it's clear Clement was attacked because of fear that he would see too much. I don't think he was in the general plan. But someone saw the possibilities and decided to hold him. Then, of course, as Clem said last night, *Redbird* was destroyed to delay search.

"I traced the steps to the back of the hangar. It was not easy. Raoul and I, however, are sure that only one person was actually concerned, and that he circled around from the field. In other words he was one of the men supposed to be searching for you, Clem. Of our suspected group, Ole and Johannes were held at camp."

"Johannes ran down to the fire right after me," said Donald, "and he worked hard on the water lines."

"Me, I think he could afford to," said Raoul. "He knew the damage had been done."

"How about tracing that knife?" asked Donald.

"I've a plan," said Walter. "If any of us showed it, suspicion might arise. I'm going to ask Black Mike to use it. He's always whittling, you know, when he's sitting about camp. He will let me know if anyone claims it, but he won't give it up. He'll just refer the person to me, saying I must have picked it up near camp."

"Worth trying," said Clement, and Raoul nodded.

"Next," went on Walter, "we must spot that flyer. Probably the weather will keep him in today. But he'll be sure to get out the first day after this storm. If he doesn't know of Clem's escape, he'll be anxious about him at that hut. He may fear he'll lack fuel or food. If he has discovered the escape, he'll wish to get in touch here, to see what is known. We must watch for the plane and try to trap him. That means a watch here at camp and one at the hut. I'll arrange that."

"How soon can Jean tell anything?" asked Donald.

"He's conscious but a bit dazed. I won't bother him for days yet," said Walter. "It's lucky, Clem, that you were not hit as hard as he. And now, Don, has any money shown up?"

"Nothing," said Donald.

"Well, that's about all of that for the moment," said Walter.

"Me, I think you must remember one thing," put in Raoul. "These men, they may yet try to kidnap you."

"I'd be a fool not to be careful, after two cases of assault," laughed Walter. "Still, Clem's escape will make 'em mighty careful. In addition, I believe that the kidnaping proposition is only an afterthought of something else.

"Listen, you guys! Dad's letters turn the light on a thing or two. For the last three months he's been having camp frictions and troubles. That's most unusual in his camps. He suspects deliberate trouble-making to reduce his production. Clem, you remember that Mr. Maguire who was mixed up with Oddie in an attempt to block our taking up an option on some timber last summer?"

"I'll say I do," laughed Clement. "I'll not soon forget our race through the wilderness to take up that option at the last minute."

"Dad suspects he's mixed up in this deal. Dad secured a contract from the Ammonoosuc Furniture Company for the spring delivery of a tremendous footage of birch, oak, and hickory. He won out by a hair over Snap Wilder. Snap Wilder is one tough hombre! Always fighting and getting licked by respectable lumbermen, but always coming up for more. His timber tracts adjoin ours, and we use the same streams in part. Chances for spring trouble there!

"Now, listen! Wilder's sore over that lost contract. He's more crooked than a snake and gives less warning when he strikes. He may have planted his men in our enlarged force. Also, as to Maguire. He's a crony of Wilder's. In addition, he's bought into the furniture company since Dad took the contract. Dad's been warned that delivery must be made on or before the minute. With winter running late and hard, that's going to be difficult. It pinches Dad two ways—delays cutting and makes the spring drive late. See?"

"As plain as my nose," said Donald.

"Now, shutting me up in that hut would disrupt this camp temporarily, and we have much of the birch Dad needs for that contract. But someone intrusted with that little stunt may have seen a chance to go farther and engineer a ransom stunt.

"It will clear up in time. The nut I am trying to crack is how to get timber out before the spring freshet. Dad is running out all he can by his private railroad. But that is four camps from us."

"Sled it down," suggested Donald.

"Remember our trip up?" grinned Walter. "No possible traveling with heavy loads, except at terrific cost."

"Any chance of a temporary extension of the railway?" asked Clement.

"Too expensive, and practically impossible in winter."

"I suggested that to get it out of the way," laughed Clement. "But Camp Fourteen, where the rails now end, is about a mile from Beaver Lake. And that lake comes to our door. How about sledding timber over the lake ice and in the one mile to the rail-head?"

"Distance, and the need of many teams for quantity hauling are the difficulties," said Walter. "We need our teams for getting timber to the rollways."

"Make a big scow, mount her on runners, and sail her down the lake," exclaimed Donald. "There's an exciting proposition!"

"I've known men to be transported that way," laughed Walter. "I'm afraid it wouldn't work with heavy loads of lumber."

"Me, I wonder if we might lay rails on that lake ice," said Raoul.

"Too expensive and difficult—that mile, especially. Surface freeze and thaw might bother, too. And you know derailments cause serious tie-ups. But——" He stopped. Suddenly his eyes lit up. "By Jove!" he exclaimed. "I believe I've got it."

CHAPTER XIII
The Pocket Knife

FOR A FEW MOMENTS Walter sat silent, evidently testing out in his mind the plan that had come to him. The others kept silent, too, while the storm roared and shrieked outside.

"For Pete's sake, spill it, Walt!" exclaimed Donald, at long last, as his impatience burst bounds.

"For Don's sake, rather!" chuckled Walter. "How's this, fellows? Dad's got a powerful caterpillar tractor he uses a lot in summer. Have it sent up to the lake. Secure a string of wood-sleds. Break a road of some sort from rail-end to lake. Set the tractor to work hauling a train of sleds from here along the lake to the railroad. It's fairly fast and could probably handle several good loads a day."

"Me, I think that's what you call 'bullee!' " exclaimed Raoul. "One leetle question, Walt. The tractor, she haul a long load down the lake. But will she carry it that one mile to the train?"

"Let her haul her limit down the lake," responded Walter. "Then she can split her load and double trips over the rough section."

"Me, I am foolish," laughed Raoul. "Of course!"

"Walt, you've hit the bull's-eye," cried Donald. "I apply, here and now, for the post of engineer on the Beaver Lake Tractor Railway."

"Suppose the tractor has a habit of breaking through the ice, Don," laughed Clement. "Will you agree to stay by the ship?"

"You don't believe she is so heavy she'll go through, do you?" exclaimed Donald, so anxiously that all roared with laughter.

"Plenty of thickness this winter to carry her," laughed Walter. "Since you folks like the plan, I'll get word out by messenger as soon as the storm lets up, and see what Dad thinks of it. Thanks a lot for your help! I don't think I'd have thought of this if it hadn't been for the discussion and the suggestions that were made."

"Can't we get the telephone wire working down the line?" said Donald, anxious, as usual, for action. "Then, if your father is in reach, you could talk with him."

Walter looked up quickly. "That's a good idea, Don. A wire gang is probably working up from Base Station and may be well along. That ice storm, however, may have wrecked things badly; and this blizzard won't improve matters. I believe Black Mike once worked on a field wire gang, and we have material here. He might start from this end. Want to go along, Don?"

"You won't need to offer twice," exclaimed Donald. "When do we start?"

"We'll let the blizzard blow itself out first," laughed Walter.

Too excited to care to turn in, the boys talked on and on until late into the night. All recent adventures were rehashed, and future possibilities were discussed at length.

In the morning all awoke to a consciousness of a bitter, searching cold working through every crack and crevice. Their ears rang, too, with the howl and shriek of a mighty gale that drove with it a blinding, swirling mass of fine snow powder. No one of the boys had ever seen a worse blizzard, and only Raoul had ever experienced one to closely approach it.

It was with the utmost difficulty that the four fought their way, in the teeth of the tempest, to the Mess Camp, although the latter was only a stone's throw away. The wind snatched their breath away, and the zero air appeared to freeze their very marrow.

Men coming from the men's camp, having the storm at their backs, in some cases were blown by the Mess Camp doors and had to claw their way back or else work in by way of the cook shack. The experience was severe enough to keep them around the tables after the meal was over. They sat about, talking of past storms and relating exciting experiences. Donald and Clement stayed on to listen.

Black Mike sat by one of the great red-hot drum stoves, whittling a piece of maple into the shape of an Indian figure. He was not without a certain crude skill in such things. From time to time men drifted over to watch him. Among these, after a time, Terry appeared. He asked to see the figure and studied it with interest and curiosity.

"Say, that's great!" he exclaimed, with genuine approval. Then, as Black Mike again began work, he broke out, "Hello! Where did you find that knife, Black Mike? It's mine. Say, you robber, when did you pick my pocket?"

Black Mike grinned, for the tone was wholly friendly. At the same time he shot the swiftest of glances at Clement, to be sure the latter was listening. "Y're one big boy, Terry, to let a man pick y'r pocket. When did it happen?"

"I dunno when or where. I missed it a day or so ago. Say, you, pass it over."

He grabbed for it, but Black Mike's great arms fenced him off. "No ye don't!" he grinned. "Me, I like this blade for carving. An' besides, the boss found this knife an' loaned it to me. See him."

Terry nodded and turned away. Clement and Donald took an early opportunity to slip out and find Walter and report to him.

"Now, just where does this leave us?" demanded Clement disgustedly. "Terry was in the group that met us out on the trail. You remember, Raoul? So he could not have been down at the hangar touching off *Redbird*."

"Unless," suggested Raoul, "he fix a clock touch-off."

"You know," said Clement, "I think Johannes recognized that knife. I think he went up to look at it rather than at the figure Black Mike was carving. And I'm sure he and Jules exchanged a glance when Terry claimed it."

"I've an idea," said Walter slowly, "that this has brought us a step forward, just the same. Let's wait and see if Terry does anything."

All that day and the day following, the blizzard raged with unabated fury. The third day, the sun broke through the clouds, but the slowly decreasing wind still piled up the drifts. Walter grew more sober with each passing day, for production was stopped. And while felling might begin again with the end of the storm, it would take days to open up trails.

Nor was this all the trouble the storm caused. At first the men had welcomed the enforced holiday. But soon close confinement began to wear on them. Men wearied of intimate contact with their fellows. Tempers flared and grouches started smouldering, to persist for the season. Now and then men clashed, and fights resulted. Moreover, a shortage of certain provisions affected the meals, despite all Little John's ingenuity. Complaints arose. Some men, led by Rostinov, urged that the giant moose, who now hung constantly around camp, should be slaughtered for food. Walter had to meet that with positive threats.

But at last, with clearing skies, the temperature went up, the snow settled under the warm sun rays, and main trails could be broken open. The men returned to work in relief, if not in good-nature, and again the "chunk-a-chunk" of axes, and the "zing" of saws, and the shouts of teamsters rang cheerily through the forest.

On the first day of open weather, Walter started Black Mike and Donald down the trail towards Camp Seventeen, laden with field telephone supplies and with letters to go on by messenger if they found little chance of opening wires through to the public lines.

"For our part," Walter said to Raoul and Clement, "we must keep the men up to the mark and at the same time watch for the mystery plane. If we see the plane, we'll watch for signals but not interfere with any that may be sent up from camp. I'm anxious for our flying friend to put in an appearance."

It was as Clement was walking in with Raoul at noon that both caught the note of the plane. They discovered it finally, flying high and over the stream that led by the rollways. Sure enough, as it sped over camp, black smoke was discharged.

"One—two—three—four—five," counted Clement. "I wonder if we should turn back and look for the return signal."

"Me, I say not," answered Raoul. "Leave that to Walt. We should not arouse suspicion in camp."

Walter came in late and busied himself with his meal. It was only after most of the woodsmen had drifted out that he had a chance to say, "Someone replied to that plane signal with five puffs. Probably an air pistol. I expect that means five o'clock. That's at dusk, shortly after our men have struck work. Raoul, you and I will go out to that pond and interview Mr. Pilot when he lands. Clement, you keep tab on the men as they return from work and try to see who come in late. But don't go off where you'll be alone and unguarded."

For all three of them the afternoon seemed to drag endlessly. But gradually the sun dropped to the horizon, and at four-forty-five the triangle gave the signal to cease work. At once men began straggling back towards camp.

Somewhat earlier, Raoul and Walter, from different points in the field, had slipped into cover and worked their way to an agreed-upon meeting place. Here Walter had a rifle concealed. With The Black Shadow at their heels, the two hastened towards the pond and at its edge concealed themselves in a dense thicket. Barely had they gained this cover when they heard the far-off beat of the plane motor and finally made out the black speck that steadily grew larger.

The pilot set the plane down neatly on its skis, taxied over the pond surface, and swung around for a take-off. Leaving his motor idling, he tossed out his own skis, swung down from the cockpit, put on the long runners, and started shoreward.

Walter shifted his position and moved out a little to meet the stranger face to face. As he did so a whistle shrilled sharply farther along the shore—two blasts, a pause, two more. Instantly the aviator wheeled about and sped desperately towards his plane.

"*Halt!*" cried Walter.

The man ran on, paying no attention. Walt fired over the man's head, but even this did not stop him.

"*Get him, Lupus!*" yelped Raoul.

The wolf dog shot away, a black streak. But the pilot, skiing desperately, had already reached the plane. He was swinging up when Lupus arrived and, with a wild leap, fastened on a ski. The man kicked it free and toppled into the cockpit. The Black Shadow ran back to gain a flying start, but already the motor was roaring and the plane starting to move. With a magnificent effort the dog got his forepaws over the edge, but was beaten off. The plane sped away and presently made an unsteady take-off.

"Me, I send Lupus after that whistler," exclaimed Raoul excitedly. He started to give the signal.

"No," snapped Walter. "That chap may be armed, and he knows Lupus and what the dog can do. He would not hesitate to shoot him. I think too much of The Black Shadow to let that happen. Let's go up and find the tracks, however. We'll trail 'em in. Those chaps were too wise for us, this time, Raoul. Instead of meeting outside camp, they arranged to meet here. The fellow on shore spotted us at the last minute."

Before long they located the tracks of a man who had come and gone from camp and who had stood at a point from which he could easily spot Walter when he moved out to intercept the pilot. The two young fellows began to follow the trail in.

"That man, he go fast," said Raoul. "And look you, Walt, he have a long stride, a very long stride. The man who tried to get you! Me, I shall watch for man who takes a long stride when he is in a hurry."

They sped along, but the man ahead had had enough of a start easily to keep his distance. Consequently, when near camp, Walter slowed down, and the two entered camp in a leisurely manner. It was already deep dusk, but as they approached the Men's Camp a man swung out the doors and came hurriedly down a path. Rounding a corner, he ran full tilt into a tremendous figure blocking the way. The man was thrown to the ground. The figure gave a hoarse, throaty snort.

The man, springing to his feet, aimed a savage blow at the tender nose of the Spirit Moose. The animal snorted again and swung around angrily. The man leaped to a near-by stump and strove to jerk free an ax that had been driven into it.

"*Stop!*" yelped Walter, springing forward.

The man swung around, revealing, in the dim light, the harsh features of Johannes. "Keep out of this, you!" he snarled. "This moose is dangerous, and I'm teaching him a lesson."

Walter leaped forward, jerked the ax from the other's hand, and tossed it backward towards Raoul. "You'll do as I say," he barked. "Let that moose alone, Johannes. Now and always! Understand?"

Their hot glances locked. Johannes's hands clenched. He crouched as if about to spring. Then his glance wavered and fell on The Black Shadow, also crouching and with lips rolled back from white fangs. "Oh, all right!" the bully growled. "But next time that moose will get his." He swung off and tramped away, passing the Spirit Moose, which wuffled—as if mockingly—and shook its great antlered head.

"Me, I think some day that moose will give Johannes all he's asking for," said Raoul.

When the two entered the Mess Camp, all except Johannes were in their seats. He came in later, sullen and ugly, snarling viciously when addressed. Jules and Rostinov eyed him questioningly and also stole glances towards the young men at the end of the table.

Later in the evening, when the chums were in their little hut, Clement reported, "Jules came into camp late, and Rostinov very late. Ole hung about some distance from the buildings as if waiting for the others. Johannes I did not see. Jules, when he came back, came from the slope where I saw the man the day I was attacked."

"The trail is warming up," said Walter. He explained about the escape of the pilot. Then he went on, "At least he left us a souvenir." He took up the ski and examined it. All at once he started and peered closer. "There are some worn initials here. They appear to be 'C. O.' And that plane looked like an Oddie plane! That 'C. O.' may stand for Charles Oddie. The son of old Decker Oddie, you know. Here's a fine mix-up."

"I'd hardly expect that old man to do this sort of thing," said Clement.

"Nor I," agreed Walter. "But the son is painted in other colors. He's both spiteful and a weakling. I——"

He stopped short as someone rapped on the door. "Come in!" he added.

Terry Connors appeared in the doorway. The usual mischievous gleam was lacking in his eyes, which were a bit uneasy. "Sorry to interrupt, Boss," he said. "The fact is I found Black Mike using a knife of mine. And when I asked for it, he said you had found it and I must apply to you."

"Where did you lose it, Terry?" asked Walter.

"Don't just know, sir!"

"When?"

"Not sure, Boss. I missed it the day the hangar was burned. But why——"

"Why am I asking all these questions?"

"Well, I was wondering." Terry eyed him sharply. "I can prove property all right. My initials are on the shank of the smallest blade."

Walter took the knife, which Black Mike had returned to him, and examined the blade. Then he had Clement and Raoul look it over, while Terry stared at them, clearly puzzled and suspicious.

"Terry," said Walter finally, "I'm not going to return this knife at present."

"And why not?" demanded Terry a little truculently. A spark of anger glowed in his eyes.

"Because this knife was found beside the burning *Redbird* almost immediately after the fire started. It was used there or dropped there by the person who broke into the hangar from the rear."

Terry started; then he reddened, and his hands clenched. And on top of that he went white. "You—you don't think *I* set that off, do you?" he demanded. "Why I—I——"

"Either you set the fire," said Walter quietly, "or someone wished to have it appear that you did."

"Well, I didn't," snapped Terry. His eyes showed both anger and uneasiness.

"Certain facts incline me to believe you," said Walter. His voice hardened. "But, Terry, are you playing square with the company that employs you? What do you know about the troubles that are going on? Your companions are none of the best, you know."

Terry hesitated, evidently fighting some inward battle. Then his gaze, avoiding Walter's, shot by the latter to the window behind him. And suddenly those eyes were fixed and staring. The others, swinging about, had a vague impression of a face fading into darkness. Raoul leaped to his feet to charge out, but Walter caught his arm and thrust him back in a chair.

"Going to tell?" asked the young boss quietly.

Terry backed towards the door. Slowly he shook his head. "I—I can't," he mumbled, turning the knob. He lunged out.

Walter started to say something but the "burr-r-r-r-ring" of an electric bell interrupted.

"The telephone!" cried Clement.

Walter leaped over and caught up the receiver. "Walter Northrop of Camp Eighteen," he exclaimed.—"Hello, Don. What's that? Through all the way? *Bully!* You and Mike have done well. Where are you?—Camp Sixteen?—You say Camp Fourteen wants me?—All right. I'll look for you two tomorrow. 'Bye!"

He broke off and rang the call for Camp Fourteen. Again he announced himself. Then his voice changed. "Why, *Dad!* Were you coming up?—Sure, I can tell you. Wait!" He swung about. "Raoul, see that I'm not disturbed or spied upon. Now, Dad. Gee! It's great to hear your voice.—I can sum up what's been going on here. After that I'll tell you of our plan for getting out birch timber before spring freshet time. Listen!"

For a half hour he retold the trouble in Camp Eighteen, stopping only to answer questions calling for further enlightenment. When that matter had been covered, he took up the transportation question. Here there was plainly argument, hot and heavy. But finally Walter rang off and then turned to the others, his eyes shining.

"We win," he cried. "The Beaver Lake Tractor Railway is agreed to. Dad was coming up. Instead, he's going back to Camp Fourteen to see that the connecting road is started instanter. The tractor and sleds will be sent up as soon as they can be gotten to the lake."

"Boy! We'll get that lumber out or bust," cried Clement, with unusual enthusiasm for him.

CHAPTER XIV
Donald, Detective

"I UNDERSTAND YOU GUYS!" exclaimed Walter. "We'll keep this transportation matter secret until the tractor actually arrives with the sleds in its train. If our trouble-makers get wind of it, we might have more mix-ups on our hands."

"Can we be doing anything to prepare for the coming of the tractor train?" asked Clement. "We'll need to deliver logs at the lake shore. And won't we need a loading platform?"

"That worries me," confessed Walter. "If we start delivering at the lake shore, these troublesters will smell a rodent. I think I'll bring our stuff out and leave it at the end of the present rollways nearest the lake. It will look as if we intend building another rollway there. I think we could bring the tractor down there with a sled at a time for the first loading. After the secret is out, we'll load at the lake."

"Count me in—and Don also," said Clement. "We can bring down a few logs at odd times, and be glad of the exercise. Doesn't your Dad offer some sort of bonus to the camp that gets out the greatest footage, Walt?"

"Yes, based on the average of men in the field. Might not be a bad thing to talk up, though we started late and have had bad weather most of the time. Our chance is slight."

"Who do you think peeked in the window and threw a scare into Terry?" asked Clement.

"One of the gang, you may be sure," returned the young boss. "Terry was scared for fear they would think he was here to squawk. I'm anxious for them to get suspicious of one another."

"Me, I have one leetle question," said Raoul. "When you talk with Big Jim, you say something about a deputy sheriff. Is it permitted that we know what is up?"

"Sure!" agreed Walter. "I asked Dad to have Black Mike deputized by the sheriff. His services might come in handy."

"If Black Mike, he lay a hand on a man, that man will feel it," chuckled Raoul. "Me, I think you do well."

Early the next evening, Black Mike tramped wearily into camp. Later he met with the four boys in the little hut, and was made familiar with the inside of the situation. Of his loyalty, now, there was no question. Besides, he was very proud of his deputyship and hoping for action. His eyes glowed when the tractor proposition was explained to him.

In a day or two trails were open and logs began to move down toward the stream. Now activities were more widespread, and oversight was necessarily less close. At once petty annoyances multiplied. Harness broke unexpectedly. Log chains and tools disappeared. A whole set of newly sharpened axes were found blunted and dull. Bad mix-ups occurred from time to time on the trails, causing delays.

Donald, during these days, was in his element. The detective fever burned within him. He was everlastingly on the watch, moving stealthily about, appearing unexpectedly where least looked for. And in the end he did help.

"Look at that, will you?" he exclaimed at one of their evening discussions, tossing down a new five-dollar bill. "It's one of a series."

"Spill it!" cried Clement.

"Owens!" responded Donald, chuckling at the other boys' surprise, "paid it in at the Wanigan Camp tonight. I asked him where he banked, that he was able to produce bills like that in the deep woods. He said he had sold something to one of the men. I didn't dare press him."

"Again a step forward," said Walter. "I think Owens is friendly, but he's a loose talker. You did right, Don, though it's too bad we don't know who paid him."

"But the great detective *does* know."

"We take off our hats to you, Mr. Sheerluck Holmes," grinned Walter. "Are we permitted to know the rest?"

"I believe I can trust you," said Donald. "After I closed the camp, I dropped into the Men's Camp and showed off Skipper. And all the time I was using my eyes. At last I saw Jules picking at a banjo. It was the banjo that Owens used to play at times. And the men were joking with him at his efforts to master it, especially as it was short a string. See?"

But the next day Donald made a discovery of much more serious import. "Walt," he said, "we're in for some kind of a blow-up, I think. I believe that the lock to the shack where you keep that supply of explosives has been tampered with. I happened to think of that place today and stopped and took a look. There are one or two fresh dents around the lock, and one tiny sliver of wood is freshly broken out."

"Phe-ew!" whistled Walter. "Fine work, Don. I'll investigate as soon as I can do it secretly. I hope it's a false alarm. Wish I could take you in with me, but I'd better slip in alone."

"That's right," agreed Donald, forcing back his disappointment. "But I'll have my eyes on things outside."

"I'm beginning to believe you," retorted Walter, grinning now.

But he did not grin when, later in the day, he slipped into the little hut back from the main camp buildings. Within was carried a small supply of black powder and of dynamite. These explosives were used in road work and in breaking jams in drives.

Walter had examined the stock after the blowing up of the rollway stack and had found it intact. Now, when he took off the heavy padlock, he gasped. The old staple had been cut away with a thin file, thus releasing the lock. Later a new staple had been fed through and driven in. A battery had disappeared and with it several sticks of dynamite.

The young boss lost no time in delays. It was important that he should not be long missing from the sight of men who were carrying guilty secrets. A few minutes' quick thought, and he went straight to Little John and Spareribs. Quietly he told what had been discovered.

"Little John," he said, "I want the Men's Camp searched for any lead. Spareribs can do it when he goes to tend the fires, but you keep watch. Report anything suspicious."

Returning to the field, he informed Raoul and Clement of the latest turn of affairs. Raoul was to slip away and select a hiding place for the remainder of the explosives, transfer them there and conceal the place. Raoul was a true forest man. He would not be caught if on his guard.

When the little group met in their private quarters that evening, the smiles had disappeared and lines of anxiety marked every face. Each one felt the overshadowing of a deadly menace.

"Spareribs has discovered a signal pistol in Jules's bunk," said Walter. "He left it undisturbed for the moment. We will get it later. He has also discovered from a paper that Johannes also goes by the name of Wilcoxen."

"Me, I hear of that chap," exclaimed Black Mike. "He make trouble in a camp up north; later he is one of Wilder's men."

"So we move on," said Walter. "The search of the Men's Camp has not been completed. It has to be done with the utmost care. As for the rest, none of us, I believe, has found any concealed explosives. Raoul, however, has chosen a hiding place for our supplies and has begun a transfer."

"It may be," said Clement, "that some word of the tractor railway has gotten through, and the gang is lying in wait for that. When do you expect the tractor, Walt?"

"The tractor ought to be along soon. I got word from Pete at Camp Seven that things were about ready. I expected definite word today. But the wire did not sound right when Pete was talking, and tonight it's dead." He forced a grin. "Looks like your work wasn't so well done, Don."

"Or," retorted Donald, "someone's tapped the wire; perhaps cut it."

Raoul signaled sharply with uplifted arm; then he pointed to the base of the door. A paper was being slipped under it. Don reached down to snatch it up. But Walter shoved him aside and sprang for the door. He jerked it open and leaped out. The others streamed after. They were in time to make out a figure streaking up the path. In time, too, to see another figure leap from behind a tree and fell the runner with a terrific blow.

"*Stop!*" yelled Walter, springing forward.

The attacker gave one backward glance; then he sprang forward and around a corner of the Men's Camp. Instantly there sounded a muffled cry and an angry snort. It was followed by a piercing scream of fear and pain.

Walter and Raoul raced side by side ahead of the others. Rounding the corner, they plowed to a halt, facing the Spirit Moose. Its antlers pinned a man against the log wall.

"Back!" ordered Raoul quietly, fearlessly stepping up to the great animal and jerking at its antlered head. The animal drew back and the man it held crumpled to the ground.

"Johannes!" exclaimed Walter, flashing on the little torch he carried. He made a quick examination. "Leg broken and badly bruised. Take him in, fellows! Now for the other chap!"

But the other fallen figure had disappeared.

"Now," said Walter, "let's see the paper." He took it and read aloud the unsigned message. " 'Serious trouble is intended. I can't tell what or where. Watch your step.' Disguised handwriting," he commented. "I'll hazard a guess. Terry! Now turn in. Clem, you're first on guard. Keep Lupus with you. Watch every instant. There's danger for anyone standing guard. Lights out!"

Clement stepped into the darkened hut at midnight, and Donald took his place. Donald insisted on Skipper in place of The Black Shadow. Skipper was a wiser and older dog than the summer before, and he would now obey orders.

A long hour had passed when Donald straightened up, tense and alert. A shadowy figure had seemed to come from the doorway of the Men's Camp and fade into the shadow of the building. Skipper growled, and Donald silenced him.

And then a second figure drifted from the Men's Camp. This one also faded into the building shadow. But presently Donald spotted it working around back of other buildings towards the lake shore. Instantly, with the utmost caution, he set out in pursuit. On the two went, with Skipper tight at Donald's heels. And presently the trailer discovered that the one person ahead had become two. They proceeded to the lake shore and on around a bend of the inlet that led to camp. Fearing discovery if he followed the same course, Donald took to the woods and cut across.

When at last he cautiously approached the lake, it was to see two men working far out on the ice. They appeared to be cutting out a small section. From this they appeared to cut a small groove towards the shore, stopping after a time to cut out another section. After that, one man disappeared into the woods and brought back some wire and a black box that Donald knew must be the missing battery. Working from the far point, they evidently set explosives and wired them up. A near-shore connection bothered, and a man jerked off a mitten and worked with bare hands.

Then the men picked up the battery and the coil of wire and started into the woods, trailing the wire as they went.

Donald edged closer and waited until the men appeared to be some distance in. Then he crawled still closer shoreward, pulled Skipper about, and pointed to the glove that still lay on the ice. "Fetch it!" he said.

"Tomorrow—or today, I guess it is—I'll be selling a pair of mittens," chuckled Donald.

Then the men came back out of the woods, brushing snow over the wires and tracks. The man who had flung his mitten aside, hunted for it and muttered oaths when he failed to find it.

"Come on," growled the other. "We've got to get back. I don't like this business."

Only after they had gone did Donald move. He went down to the point where the wires came ashore, and followed these in. Then getting out his heavy jackknife, he cut them. Some fifty feet farther inland he cut the wires again. Finally he traced them to a dense fir; and under this he found the battery with the plunger all ready. One shove for contact and the ice across the inlet would have shattered into a thousand pieces.

Donald debated taking in the battery. Then he decided against it. "It's a trap," he told himself delightedly, "and they've set it to catch themselves."

CHAPTER XV
The Clear-Up

FIFTEEN MINUTES LATER DONALD was speaking to Walter, who had roused and was uneasy about his chum's late return. After a minute, he waked the others, and all listened eagerly as the story unfolded.

"You've put it over for sure, Don," said Walter, when the tale ended. "It was risky, but the results seem to have justified that risk. Now, here's my plan. I think it's evident the gang proposes to blow up the ice under the tractor when it comes along. Very good! Black Mike will be shown where the battery is placed. Don will stay on guard at camp. Since he spends much time here, that will arouse no question. When the tractor is sighted, Little John will ring the triangle, so that all men will tramp down. Until then, one of us will be watching each of the three left—Ole, Jules, and Rostinov.

"I consider Terry out of it, though we'll keep an eye on him. When the alarm triangle rings, Black Mike will slip off and hide near the battery. The rest of us will watch to check on the man who slips off to go to it. Also, at earliest dawn, I'll send Black Mike out to look over the wires near camp. Now get what sleep you can. No need to watch further tonight!"

In the morning when it could be safely done, Walter passed out several bits of information. "I slipped off with Black Mike," he began, "though we sneaked back separately and from different directions. Our telephone wire, we found, had been tapped a little distance out and run under a dense spruce. Plenty of signs there of a man hiding. Also, evidently later, the wire had been cut farther out. To avoid suspicion, we left things as they were. I think, however, we may expect the tractor today.

"Now another thing! Little John reports that Johannes was feverish last night and was constantly muttering about Jules and Rosty—short for Rostinov. Ole's name was not mentioned. That seems reasonable. Ole's stupid, not a leader. They may use him; that's all. Now, fellows, hop to it. The crucial day is with us."

Clement was delayed in camp working on his books. As he was ready to leave, Donald came in.

"Tell Walt," he chuckled, "that our friend Jules stopped in to buy a pair of mittens. Said his others had worn out. I've asked Spareribs to try to locate the other old one. If they match—oh, boy!"

The men tramped in for the hot noon meal and departed once more for work. For perhaps the twentieth time Donald went down to the lake shore. And this time he imagined he heard a faint note that sounded like a motor. He listened; presently he thought to drop to the ice and put his head close to the surface. Instantly his ear caught the unmistakable note.

Leaping to his feet, he tore madly down the inlet and around the bend. Far off down the lake a long, dark something was moving slowly his way. Whirling about, Donald made tracks for camp. As he came within hailing reach, he yelled, "Whale the triangle, Little John! *Quick!*"

Little John came lumbering out the door of the cook shack. He bent to grasp the great maul. The triangle leaped and rang under his mighty blows. From up the woods trail, presently, men came streaming, led by Clement. Walter brought up the rear. Still the clangor of the triangle continued.

Clement guided his pack of questioning men straight by the camps and out on the inlet ice, and then on to the bend. Then, indeed, came excited yells, for the rattling tractor, with its string of a half dozen sleds, could now be clearly made out. No need to tell those woodsmen what that contraption meant. They began to scurry out to meet it. Rostinov and Ole and a few others remained.

"Jules!" murmured Walter in Clement's ear, nodding towards the woods, and then he immediately went on. Clement looked about. Black Mike was not to be seen.

The clangor of the triangle stopped. Little John was rolling down the slope to join the reception committee. And then Clement was able to catch the snarling mouthings of men in combat, coming from the woods. Rostinov heard too. He swung about and ran for the woods farther down shore.

"*Get him, Lupus!*" yelled Raoul.

The Black Shadow leaped forward as if shot from a gun. Rostinov saw him coming and drew a heavy knife. But Lupus was not caught napping. He feinted one way, drew a slashing stroke, leaped above the stabbing arm and crashed the man to the ice. With the animal's teeth at his throat, Rostinov dared not move.

The men on the train stared at the sight. And they stared again when Black Mike and Walter came out of the woods, thrusting Jules ahead of them. The latter and Black Mike were decidedly the worse for wear.

Among the first to swing from the forward sled was a magnificently pro-portioned man, at least six feet three in height. His hair was dark brown; his eyes were wide set and gray, and keen as a hawk's. His jaws were firm, his smile attractive; and his voice was both friendly and compelling as he greeted man after man. Big Jim had arrived.

"Welcome, Dad!" cried Walter.

Then Big Jim was shaking hands with the chums and with Black Mike.

At once his expression sobered and he whipped around on his son. "Say, boss," he demanded, "what's the meaning of this exhibition?" His eyes flashed from Jules to Rostinov. "Can't you keep order among your men?"

"We *are* keeping it, sir," grinned Walter. "These men intended to celebrate your arrival by blowing up the tractor train. You'll have the facts, sir, this afternoon. I—what's that plane?" He pointed to the north.

"I expect it's Oddie," said Big Jim. "I asked him to drop in here for a conference."

Walter and Clement exchanged glances. "I think," said the former, "that we have business with his chauffeur. Clem, get that ski."

Clement nodded. When he returned the plane had landed and massive old Denton Oddie was climbing out. He walked with Big Jim while Walter and Clement tramped over to the plane.

"Hello!" greeted young Oddie coldly. He appeared uneasy. His glances were taking in Rostinov and Jules.

"Thought I'd ask if this ski was yours," said Walter, holding up the ski.

Oddie's cheeks flushed. "Why, I don't remember losing that," he lied. Then, seeing Clement climbing up to look into the forward cockpit, he snarled, "Hey, get down out of that!"

"Check again, Walt," said Clement, dropping back. "When I was carried off, I rubbed one boot back and forth inside there, to make an X. You can see my mark."

"Kidnaping is a serious job, Oddie," snapped Walter. "And if Clem had been caught out in that hut in the blizzard, unable to get out for fuel, murder might have been added. We can prove—"

"Don't," gasped Oddie. "I didn't want to mix in that—I was forced to do it."

"There'll be a hearing in an hour or so," said Walter coldly. "You'll come across with the facts at that time, or I won't answer for the consequences. That's your only chance."

Two hours later there was a gathering in one end of the Men's Camp. The chums and Black Mike, Big Jim, Oddie and his son, Johannes, Jules, Ole, Terry, Rostinov, Little John and Spareribs were all present.

Definitely and clearly Walter stated the facts that all the chums knew. He then threw on the table the mitten that Skipper had retrieved from the ice.

After that he called on Spareribs to produce a mitten he had found in Jules's bunk. All could see that it paired with the first.

"I'll talk," shrieked Jules. "That man—" he pointed a trembling finger at Rostinov—"he make me. He threatened to kill me."

"You can talk later," snapped Walter. "Oddie, what have you to say?"

"Is my son in this?" gasped old Denton.

"I'm sorry, sir," said Walter.

"Spill everything, son," growled Denton.

"There's not much," mumbled young Oddie. "I carry mail and messages for our camps. On the side, I did it for Wilder. He found I disliked Walter and suggested making a little trouble to put Walter in wrong. Out of spite, I agreed. Then I found he had planted a regular gang in the Northrop Camps, headed by Rostinov."

"How did Rostinov communicate down the line?" demanded Walter.

"Tapped wires and messages I picked up or left at concealed points on pond shores near the camps. Rostinov, through Jules, got me to take some money. I—I didn't want to, but I'd got in debt and was afraid Dad would find it out. Rostinov made me take Osgood away. Threatened my life if I didn't."

"Who struck down Jean and Clement?"

"Jules dropped Jean; Rostinov, Osgood. Rostinov planned to get you during the search for Osgood, but was scared off. He always kept in the background. Rostinov was engineering the kidnaping on his own hook."

"Rostinov," put in Walter, "is a militant Red. Papers just discovered in his belongings prove that. We have checked on him, too, by a fragment torn from his Mackinaw when he tried to ambush me, and by his long stride. All right, Oddie. Now, Terry, want to talk?"

"Ready, sir!" said Terry. And talk he did—straight to the point. He knew young Oddie and had agreed to be a trouble-maker just for the fun of it.

Jules and Johannes followed. Both were ready to talk in order to lessen their own punishment. They proceeded to heap blame on the sullen, glowering Rostinov. They also gave away the names of men in the ring, serving in other camps. Ole, it appeared, was used a little without really knowing it.

"A great clean-up, son!" exclaimed Big Jim. "Oddie—" he turned to old Denton—"we'll hold your son only as a witness, also Terry, here. But I think you and I have enough on Wilder to run that crooked stick out of the company of honest lumbermen. That's really what I wished to see you about. Now, about this tractor—"

"*Geewillikers!*" cried Walter. "I actually forgot the tractor train. Court's adjourned." He bolted for the door.

The last day of February, weeks ahead of spring freshet time, and yet the streams were roaring. No good, though, to start a drive! A night's freeze at this changeable season, and things might jam. The ice grew softer. Walter debated with his friends the question of trying the last load.

"One big load gets out our contract stuff."

"Let her go," said Clement. "If she goes through the ice, the logs will float and can be rescued."

"Load up!" snapped Walter to Black Mike, and the other nodded.

They pulled away at midday, the sun so warm they shed their coats. Walter took a slightly new course, to avoid a possible weakening of the old track from constant use. But the tractor left deep ribbons of trail behind her. Even the sleds cut deep. They slowed down progress.

They were well out from the shore and over halfway on their course when the crackling reports of the splitting ice surface became very noticeable. Walter eyed the nearest shore. No, it wouldn't do to turn in. It was very warm in on that edge. The ice would be weaker. Keep going!

Crack! Crack!

Then it happened. The tractor simply crashed through without warning. Walter had no time to jump. For an instant the others saw his body, then cakes of ice slid over. And then he was up, struggling feebly towards something that would bear his weight.

"Wait," snapped Raoul, as Donald and Clement flung themselves forward. "It's up to Lupus."

He looped the rope in the dog's collar. "Get Walter," he ordered.

The intelligent beast leaped forward, ran to the edge of the firm ice and sprang over to the broken cakes. Then, with a mighty leap, he landed in the water beside the young boss and caught the shoulder of his coat in his great teeth.

Walter turned and snatched the rope. Even the slight support of the swimming dog helped. Despite the deadening chill of the icy water, he managed to slip the rope around himself. Then Raoul and Clement drew him in and helped him onto what was left of hard pan.

"Run for the shore, Walt," cried Raoul. "*Everybody* run!"

"A two-hundred-yard dash!" gasped Donald, as they sprinted, leaped gaps, slid and skidded to safety, while the ice broke behind them. But they made it. Then they looked back. The tractor was out of sight, but the timber load showed just at the surface.

The next day the four returned to Camp Eighteen, after having arranged for the rescue of the tractor and timbers. And then the work of getting out other timber went on. Bitter weather came; then, after weeks, a real break-up. Again the streams roared. White water showed everywhere. The ice went out.

One day the men gathered on the rollways. There was not so much timber to go. Jean, again in shape, was to handle the drive with a dozen men. Black Mike was to take over the camp for further work. For the chums, the working holiday was at an end.

"*By gar!*" came a bellow from the camp buildings. "*Whoopee-ee!*"

"Zee telephone," squeaked Little John, "she say we win ze bonus. Me, I done it, with ze gur-r-r-rand meals I cook. *Hunh?*"

"Ye boaster!" roared Spareribs. "Who did the real work? *I* did."

A familiar set-to started, but the boys did not hear. They were shaking hands all around the circle.